THE RAKE'S INSATIABLE BRIDE

CAROLINE LEE

COPYRIGHT

OTHER BOOKS BY CAROLINE LEE

Want the scoop on new books? Join Caroline's Cohort, an exclusive reader group! Or sign up for my mailing list by texting "Caroline" to 42828 to get started!

Steamy Scottish Historicals:
Those Kilted Bastards (4 books)
Bad in Plaid (6 books)
The Hots for Scots (8 books)
Highlander Ever After (3 books)
The Sinclair Jewels (4 books)
The Highland Angels (5 books)

Sensual Historical Westerns:
Black Aces (3 books)
Sunset Valley (3 books)
Everland Ever After (10 books)
The Sweet Cheyenne Quartet (6 books)

Sweet Contemporary Westerns
Quinn Valley Ranch (5 books)

River's End Ranch (14 books)
The Cowboys of Cauldron Valley (7 books)
The Calendar Girls' Ranch (6 books)

Click **here** to find a complete list of Caroline's books.

*Sign up for Caroline's Newsletter to receive exclusive content and freebies, as well as first dibs on her books! Or if newsletters aren't your thing, follow her on **Bookbub** for a quick, concise new release alert every time she publishes a book!*

ABOUT THIS BOOK

She'll do things her way, or not at all...and that includes marriage!

Industrialist Jade Thacker is used to being in control of her own life. Which is why it's damned *galling* to learn her well-meaning guardian plans to marry her off before she comes into full control of her inheritance! And a betrothal is one thing, but what's this nonsense about *marriage-by-proxy*? Is she married, or isn't she?

Well, there's one thing she can still control: her virginity. Which is why she visited London's most infamous male courtesan to rid herself of that pesky detail. But now, staring (horrified) up at the gorgeous man her possible-husband turned out to be, she's reconsidering the whole scheme.

Loving women is one of the few things he's good at...but he can't forget her!

Life was going just fine—women, wine, more women—until Cameron MacKay's father sent him that blasted letter. He loves the dear old coot, of course, but *marriage?* Especially a marriage-by-proxy? *Please*, this isn't the fourteenth century! But when he opens the door to see the (horrified) expression on the face of his most recent client, Cam admits himself intrigued.

And now the one thing she wants...is him!

Cam knows why Jade doesn't want to be married, but when a deluge strands them together in his cottage, she decides on a new goal: him. Or maybe it's just that now she's tasted the pleasure he can offer her, she wants more. Either way, he's going to have to be the strong one in this crisis.

Too bad he'll always be a rake at heart.

Warning: There's nothing "too bad" about being a rake, right? Especially a rake stuck in a forced-proximity, oh-no-there's-only-one-bed, fighting-his-own-best-interests sort of situation! This one starts super spicy and continues that way, and is full of laugh-out-loud bits you've come to expect from one of Caroline's Victorian RomComs.

CHAPTER 1

MISS JADE THACKER wasn't the shy and retiring type. She reminded herself of this as her knuckles hesitated to make contact with the hotel door.

It didn't help.

Perhaps I need to remind my knuckles of the fact.

That didn't help either.

The longer you stand here, the more foolish you look.

And the greater chance she might be discovered.

But still, she hesitated.

The step she was about to make—well, the *knock*—was bolder, and one might argue *madder,* than anything she'd done before. But Miss Jade Thacker had long ago become used to being seen as bold and perhaps a bit mad.

Besides, if you would just hurry up and get out of this hotel corridor, where anyone might see you and wonder why *a young unmarried miss is about to knock on a rake's private door, there will be considerably less chance anyone would ever learn of this.*

Before she could talk herself out of it, her knuckles rapped against a stranger's door.

From inside came a baritone call: *"Un instant, s'il vous plait."*

French? The man she'd come to see was supposed to be Scottish. That was what he was called, after all: The Scot. Was it possible he was actually French, and "Scot" was a given name? The Scots and the French had a long history of alliances, but Jade was certain Honoria's sister, Lady Melton, had said this man spoke with a delightful brogue.

Frowning, she considered the ramifications. Surely she hadn't accidentally rapped on the wrong door? *That* would be embarrassing, especially when it came time to explain why she was there.

And then the door opened, and Jade found herself fervently praying she wasn't wrong, because *ai-ya*, this man was gorgeous!

Blond curls swept across his forehead and hid his ears, blue eyes twinkled with mischief...and then he smiled, and Jade was almost certain she'd died and gone to heaven, because the vision before her had *dimples*. Two of them, mismatched on either side of that smile, which made him seem so much more touchable.

Not that you needed any excuses to touch the man, not if he's the one you've come to see.

Her fingers were already itching to brush that curl from his forehead, so she curled them into fists at her sides.

Apparently, he'd decided he'd had enough of standing in his doorway smiling at her, because in that delightfully low voice, he purred, "Good evening," in perfect English.

Not French, then.

Unable to control herself, her gaze dropped from that smile—his teeth were remarkably even and white, weren't they? Did he use some sort of special cleaning regimen to get results like that?—to the man's smooth jaw. She'd always been partial to a strong jaw, and she could likely stare at this one for a month or two.

It was natural for her eyes—currently caressing a man's

bare skin—to drop to his neck. With a shock, she realized he was wearing a dressing gown, a silk banyan in the same beautiful shade of blue as his eyes, over his shirt. Which was open at the collar, revealing the most tantalizing patch of golden skin.

In fact, the robe was tied lightly, as if he'd thrown it on to answer her knock, and she could see he'd rolled up his shirt sleeves, revealing intriguingly muscular forearms beneath the silk. And lower...

His feet were bare.

Ai-ya, had she ever considered a man's bare feet before? These were strong and wide and it was somehow intimate, to see them like this. She wondered if his hands would look similarly strong, and how they'd *feel*.

It wasn't until he cleared his throat that her gaze snapped up, and she realized she'd been standing at his hotel room door, ogling the man's *feet*.

Not your best moment, Jade.

Feeling a blush climbing from around her high-necked blouse, she did her best to lift her chin and find the steel which usually infused her spine. She'd made grown men quake when she glared at them, invoices and shipping schedules in hand. Why couldn't she find some of that steel right now?

"Good evening," she managed. "I am looking for The Scot."

"Ye've found him, milady." Oh, he really did have the most delightful brogue, did he not? "Come in, so we might become better acquainted."

It was a command, but given in such teasing tone, she couldn't bristle. Besides, he winked at her, and Jade suspected she might follow him off a short pier if he did it again.

In a bit of a daze, she stepped into the stranger's hotel room, and heard the door close behind her.

Swallowing, she turned to face the robed man. "I am—"

He stepped closer, until the blue silk covering his chest was only inches from her, and Jade slammed her mouth shut.

"Nae names, milady," he said smoothly, an easy grin tugging one corner of his lips. "I ken why ye're here, and there's nae need for me to ken anything more. Besides"—his shrug was fluid and graceful—"if ye tell me yers, I'll have to tell ye mine."

No names. Well, that certainly made things simpler. "And you..." She cleared her throat, trying to pretend she wasn't affected—intimidated, *aroused*—by the man standing so close to her. "And you do not want to tell me your name?"

Another graceful shrug, and he lifted a hand to her neck, fingertips brushing at one of the wispy strands of hair she could never seem to keep tucked into her bun. While she was busy shivering at his casual touch, he answered.

"There's a chance ye and I might meet at some function, milady. I think, with what we're about to share, anonymity might serve us better."

Her mind had turned to complete mush. Likely because his fingers were still on her skin, the soft spot below her ear. He wasn't caressing or stroking, but merely touching, in the most horribly intimate manner. No one had ever touched her there—not even her maid—and the fact this *stranger* did so...

She swallowed, trying to regain her equilibrium. "I would think, sir, if we were to be paired together at a country dance, or meet at a musicale, or attend the same political rally, we would have no trouble recognizing each other, and thus our lack of knowledge of each other's names would prove irrelevant." Her chin rose, as she tried to ignore his touch. "Besides, I'm not a lady."

His smile wasn't teasing this time, but...*impressed*? "A political rally?"

"Well, I cannot very well choose someplace as an example

where I might *actually* be, can I?" *The docks. The shipping office. My townhome.*

Her response surprised a chuckle out of him, and his hand fell away from her neck. Before she could be disappointed, though, she felt his fingers twine through hers.

Ai-ya, he was *good* at this *being intimate with someone he didn't know* thing, wasn't he?

That's his job, bai-chi!

The reminder of why she was there was sobering.

And perhaps she would be sobered enough to make her excuses and back right out of his hotel room, had he not lifted her hand to his lips then.

"If I cannae call ye *milady*, ye'll need another name. Darling? Sweetheart?" His eyes twinkled as he brushed a kiss across her knuckles. "Honey? I am partial to sweet things."

In a swift movement, he flipped her hand over, and, lips a millimeter from the sensitive skin of the inside of her wrist, above her short gloves, murmured, "Dumpling?" He held her gaze as his breath teased her skin. "Muffin?"

Look, knees, this isn't a great time to give out.

Jade sucked in a breath, and struggled to stay upright instead of allowing herself to melt into a pile of nonsense. It was a battle, as she realized she was leaning closer to this man, her pulse pounding in anticipation of feeling his lips against her skin.

"Raspberry tart?" she managed to croak. "Pudding? Sugar?"

His grin flashed right before he pressed a kiss to her wrist. Jade's eyes fluttered shut.

"Kitten," she whispered, trying to maintain a semblance of control. "Lovebird. Piglet."

In a sudden movement, the man straightened, a laugh bursting from his lips. "Piglet?" His blue eyes sparkled, his dimples deep as he shook his head. "Ye're mocking my attempts at seduction!"

Attempts? Jade's erratic pulse and the way she pressed her thighs together beneath her skirts attested to his very successful *attempts.*

She swallowed. "I was merely trying to help."

"Piglet," he repeated with a disbelieving chuckle, as his free hand landed on her hip.

She wasn't certain if he tugged her closer or if he took a step nearer, but the result was the same; Jade ended up plastered against the length of him, and *oh Lord*, but it felt good.

He felt good.

She had to tilt her head back to hold his gaze, but it was worth it; she couldn't seem to make herself look away from the laughter in those blue eyes. He seemed to be enjoying himself in a carefree way she'd never managed.

"Treasure," he whispered.

Oh, whoops, it seemed as if she *could* look away from his eyes, if only as far as his lips. They were wide and expressive, and she wondered how they'd feel on *other* parts of her.

Her brows drew in as she'd realized he'd said something. "What?"

"Treasure," he repeated, his other arm snaking around behind her. "Ye're a treasure, and I'm calling ye such."

Treasure. It was his name for her, instead of kitten or sweetheart or dumpling?

Jade found herself smiling.

"Och, there ye are." His lips pulled wide in response. "I was beginning to think I'd lost my touch."

There was a hardness pressing against her pelvis, and Jade resisted the urge to squirm. "Considering our respective positions, I doubt that very much."

The man blinked, then tilted his head back and laughed. She was mesmerized by the sight of the muscles of his neck, corded and golden, working under the lamplight. He had the same build as one of the sailors on her ships, or a fighter at her club.

He was magnificent.

And, judging from the way his movement had sent his hips pressing forward, as aroused as she was.

She might be a virgin, but she wasn't an innocent. She knew what that hardness was, pulsing against her, causing her core to thrum in eager tandem.

If The Scot was everything Honoria's sister Melanie claimed, Jade would soon see—*touch*, feel—that hardness. It would be *in* her, divesting herself of the last trappings of propriety, making her her *own* master.

Mistress.

Whatever.

The point was: *A Harlot's Guide to the Forbidden and Delightful Arts* had always been quite instructive, and Jade felt she had a fairly good grasp of the mechanics. But this arousal, this *need*, was a new experience entirely.

Excellent. That's what she needed; an experience. An experience to hold in her memory, so many years from now, when she was Lady Buthert.

No. Do not think of Jered, not now.

She hadn't entirely given up on finding a way out of this mess, after all.

Perhaps Uncle Argus will change his mind about the necessity of marriage.

She almost snorted. Her guardian's letter had been *quite* definite.

"Treasure? Ye've stopped breathing. Surely ye're no' so overwhelmed by my presence?"

Since the man had flexed his hips again, ensuring Jade felt all of his arousal, she understood his wry tone. Matching it, she raised a brow and forced herself to push aside all thoughts that weren't *here, now, tonight.*

"Your 'presence'? Modest, are you?"

A laugh burst free of his lips again, and she felt herself smiling in response.

"Lass," he murmured, one large hand splayed across her lower back to hold her in place, while the other rose to her neck. "I'd verra much like to kiss ye. Will ye allow me?"

Her breath caught again. He was *asking* her permission? She'd spent the years since her father's death crossing words—and sometimes blades—with men who saw her as lesser, unequal. And here was a courtesan, *asking* her permission.

"Please," she breathed.

His lips tugged into a grin as they lowered to hers.

THIS WAS *NOT* A NORMAL ASSIGNATION.

For one thing, most of Cam's patrons were older women, married, bored, desperate. For another, he *knew* them, and was careful with whom he chose to spend an evening of pleasure. It had been a while since he'd accepted a new client, and he'd only done so tonight because Lady Melton had arranged the meeting, and he trusted his old friend.

But this lass was *not* what he'd expected.

When Melanie had written him, explaining her sister's friend was searching for an evening of pleasure, he'd almost denied her. He had no business deflowering virgins, and Melanie should've realized that. She knew of his vow; all of his clients did, even if they chose not to speak of it.

And it wasn't as if he needed this woman's money. But if the wealthy ladies of Society were willing to lower themselves to be fooked by a Scottish bastard, then by God he was going to make them pay for it.

But he'd been intrigued enough to agree to meet the lady—

or rather, the *miss*—in his usual room at The Savoy. And now, he was certainly glad he'd made that decision.

Because this treasure he'd found had set his blood afire in a way no other woman had.

Perhaps it was the strength he saw in her, beneath her blushes. Or perhaps it was her wit, which had made him laugh several times already as he crafted his usual seduction around her.

Or perhaps it's the way she kisses, ye complete fooking idiot.

Och, aye, that was it.

He was a man who used kisses and smiles and whispers in the bedroom, the way he used lunges and ripostes and parries at his club. They were tools for accomplishing a goal.

But *this* kiss...when she whimpered softly, her lips pliant beneath his, he froze, cursing himself for moving too fast with an untried virgin. But then her arms came up, and rested on his shoulders, and he realized she was *embracing* him.

Holding him.

Pulling him closer.

And his cockstand was absolutely fine with the situation.

Grinning against her lips, he took control again, teasing her, playing with her, showing her how he liked to kiss and be kissed in return. She tasted like all his favorite desserts, but he couldn't pinpoint exactly *why*. His tongue traced the seam of her lips, and she made a soft, eager sound as she welcomed him inside.

An enthusiastic learner, indeed.

Perhaps there were benefits to accepting an untutored client.

Really, he was being *helpful*, teaching her how to kiss, wasn't he? It was his civic duty, to show her exactly how much pleasure could be found between a man's and a woman's lips. So when she left him, sated and happy, she'd have understanding of desire, and fulfillment, and what exactly a man's mouth was capable of.

He was doing his good deed for the week, really.

The fact he was going to bloody well enjoy it was an added bonus.

Her fingers twined through the curls at the back of his neck, and Cam was surprised to feel himself shiver. When was the last time he'd been so affected by an innocent response? He was rock-hard already, and the fact she wasn't practiced didn't seem to matter at all to his body.

He wanted her, plain and simple.

Lucky him.

Knowing his lips were talented—they'd had much practice, after all—he moved his kisses to the corner of her mouth, then to her jaw, nibbling just lightly, enough to make her suck in a sudden breath, then let it out on a moan, which filled him with pride.

And *that's* when she rocked her hips forward, cradling his cock with her softness, rubbing her pelvis against him in the age-old quest for fulfillment...and damned if his knees didn't suddenly go weak at the sudden burst of nearly uncontrollable desire.

He was beginning to suspect it was going to be very, very hard to stick to his vow with this little steel-edged treasure.

Straightening, he forced his breathing under control as he held her, watching her slowly blink and come back to herself.

God Almighty, but she was beautiful. He might not have said that, were they to meet at some Society event—or, what had she said? A business meeting? Nay, a political rally. She wasn't a flashing sort of beauty, all paint and primping, the kind who usually caught his eye.

This treasure was quiet, understated, self-assured. And there was definitely a beauty in that.

Her hair was black and straight, pulled back in what had

been a severe coiffure, but now was mussed. Her eyes were gray, and tilted at the corners in a way which reminded him of one of his fencing masters when he'd been a lad. As they slowly blinked open, he smiled down at her.

"Ye really are a treasure, are ye no'?"

His compliment flustered her, he could tell. Or perhaps it was because he was currently standing half-naked in a hotel room, embracing her.

One of the two.

Before she could respond to his rhetorical question, Cam decided to further the seduction. He wanted this woman with a strength he hadn't felt in a long while, but duty first.

In a sudden movement, he dropped his hold on her and stepped away, pleased to see her sway, but maintain her balance. Reaching the drinks cart in front of one of the curtained windows, he debated between the brandy and whisky.

He settled on brandy, because he was most definitely in the mood for something sweet, and poured her a measure. Taking a larger one for himself—both glasses in one hand—he turned back to reach for her hand. He saw the confusion in her eyes as he led her to the sofa, and it didn't lessen when he sat down, tugging at her.

She landed in his lap, exactly where he wanted her to be.

Her firm bottom cradled his cockstand as if it were completely natural, and when she wriggled into a more comfortable position, his knuckles tightened around the crystal to keep him from groaning.

"Now what?" she asked quietly, not looking at him. Instead, she stared at the dark liquid in her glass, cradling it in both hands. "I assume there's some sort of order to this?"

His lips twitched. "There is. But usually I have some idea of who my partner is."

A sharp gaze cut his way, then back. "You said you didn't need to know my name."

"And I dinnae." He settled against the sofa, one hand resting on her hip, holding her in place, as he sipped at his brandy. "But I dinnae ken *ye*. I dinnae ken what ye like, or what ye need."

"I thought Lady Melton explained—"

He interrupted with a smile. "Why no' tell me yerself, lass? Why have ye come to me?"

Her gaze still on her brandy, she grinned ruefully, just a quick flash of teeth. For the first time, Cam saw the slight reddening of her skin along her jaw, where his stubble had scraped at her.

He should've felt guilty, he knew. But his first, instinctive response was pride, that he'd marked her as *his*, if only for a night.

This was a new sensation, and one he'd have to examine. Later. When his lap wasn't full of delicacies.

When she exhaled, he felt her spine unbend just slightly, and his fingers pressed into her hip, letting her know she could relax into him, if she wanted.

It seemed to work, and he was surprised how peaceful he felt in that moment, sipping brandy and softly petting a beautiful woman. Her attention had landed on the copy of *A Harlot's Guide to the Forbidden and Delightful Arts,* which he tended to bring with him on his assignations, along with a few helpful accessories he wondered if he'd need tonight.

His guest didn't seem particularly surprised by the book, and he wondered if she'd seen it before. He wondered if she'd *read* it before.

Intriguing.

The moment stretched, and he felt her shift against him. Because she was uncomfortable? Or did she feel the way his cock strained against her, and know what that meant?

"I am to be married," she blurted.

A pang of—of *something* shot down his throat into his chest. He'd spent plenty of time with married women. That was, in fact, what he was known for. But he'd momentarily forgotten Melanie's explanation letter, and the reminder was a twinge of jealousy he didn't want to examine at that moment.

"Congratulations." He managed to sound unaffected.

But he caught her wince, just before she raised the glass to her lips. She sipped at the brandy like someone used to its potency.

With a sigh, she relaxed further. "I am not pleased about it, sir, so I won't accept the congratulations. I am used to being in control of my life, and I have successfully managed the business my father left me upon his death. But in order to expand it, I need money. The silent partner I recently took on is enough to keep us afloat—although I hate the fact I had to turn to someone else—but I need more."

"Hence the marriage?" he guessed.

To his surprise, she snorted softly, staring down at the glass in her hand. "The opposite. Upon my birthday next month, I will receive a substantial inheritance, set aside by my maternal grandfather. I hope to be able to buy out my partner, as soon as I can learn his name, and the rest will be more than enough to build the business into what I want it to be."

Cam hadn't expected to be enjoying this discussion quite so much, especially when he was distracted by the feel of her in his arms. But he *was*; she was an intriguing young woman. "You sound as if you have it all figured out," he murmured, as he stroked up one side of her spine.

"I did, except…" She blew out a breath, then took an extra-large sip of the brandy. "There is a man—a lord—who needs money. I do *not* wish to marry him, but he believes marrying me, before I come of age to gain my inheritance, will grant him control over it. And my business. He is...quite the nuisance."

She hadn't looked at Cam during the recitation; was in fact pretending great interest in her drink. Cam found himself not only interested in her story, but affected by the defeat he heard in her voice. He stretched to place his half-consumed glass on the table beside them, freeing both his hands to touch her.

Which he did.

"Will it?" he murmured, resting one hand gently on her thigh. "Give him control of yer business?"

Her eyes flashed toward him once. "Yes. I don't like the idea of *anyone* having control, besides me, even if he weren't a spoiled lordling who plans to destroy all my father and I have built, for his own gain."

"Ah." Cam tried a charming grin. "An heiress.."

She seemed to bristle, her spine straightening once more, her chin coming up as she met his eyes. "I brought you your payment." She reached for a pocket at her waist, fumbling with a man's wallet, as if to remind them she was the paying client here, while he was just a courtesan.

He stilled her hand, then took it, twining his fingers through hers, as his thumb traced small circles on her hip. "Time enough for that later, lass," he murmured. He was beginning to think it would be a crime to accept payment for the pleasure he was about to experience with this woman. "Tell me more about what ye need."

She watched him for a moment longer, and he saw her eyes lighten to a gray which seemed to contain shades of blues and even greens. Changeable eyes, as mysterious as their owner.

But then she exhaled and looked back to her drink. "My guardian—well, the man who oversees my inheritance—has decided I am to be married, despite my protests. He believes—and I suspect I agree, although I would never admit that to him—that the lord I mentioned before will attempt to force my hand before my birthday."

The way his gut clenched at the thought of this woman being forced into marriage by an entitled arse was entirely unreasonable. He didn't know her; he shouldn't have any opinion on her future!

Her gaze was still on her drink, and her tone speculative—and somehow defeated—when she explained, "In order to keep me safe from that lord, my uncle has decided to proactively marry me to someone of his choosing. A relative of his I've never met, but heard nothing good about."

Cam hummed. "And ye dinnae trust yer guardian to choose someone more suitable?"

"I trust him to manage my inheritance up until my birthday," she said curtly, then lifted her glass to down the rest of her brandy in one swallow. "But not in this. I *will* fight him on it. I do not *want* to be forced to marry, either to a spoiled lordling who wants me only for my father's empire, nor to a lazy layabout who'll not challenge me."

"Ah," he drawled, using his hold on her hip to tug her closer to him. When she—almost reluctantly—settled against him, he smiled. "I begin to understand. Ye are a self-made, self-assured, self-confident woman."

She stilled, then shrugged one shoulder. "I can't tell if you are mocking me, but yes. I'll accept those terms as compliments. If you have a problem with me...?"

"On the contrary, lass," he murmured, turning her hand in his so he could stroke her palm. "I am impressed by yer passion. Just the fact ye sought me out tells me ye're the kind of woman who kens what she wants."

Her face was inches from his, and her eyes flashed back and forth as she studied him, as if searching for some hint of untruth.

Hoping to convince her of his sincerity, Cam spread his

large hand across her side, then her back, stroking through her simple silk blouse and corset. He dropped her hand and splayed his across her belly, the edges of his fingers brushing the undersides of her breasts.

She shivered, and he didn't let her see him smile.

"Ye dinnae want to be married?" he prompted in a murmur. "So ye came to me."

Her nod was jerky, and he noticed her breathing had quickened. "I…" She swallowed, still holding his gaze. "I want this to be on *my* terms. I want to be the one to decide who takes my virginity. Not a man who uses his power and social standing to bully me into marriage, not some cousin I've never met…but *me*." Her voice had dropped to a whisper, her eyes still on his. "I want to feel pleasure once, in case I never feel it again."

"Impossible," he whispered in return, ignoring the way his chest ached from holding back the rage at this woman casually mentioning her sale to another man.

Tonight she's yers. Just for tonight. Make it count.

"Impossible?" she repeated.

Trying to understand, himself, even as he explained to her, Cam allowed his hand to creep up her belly to her chest. Bypassing her small breasts—for a change—he settled his palm over her heart, his fingers splayed wide.

"Impossible, because after tonight, lass, ye'll ken pleasure." He swallowed, wondering if he was making any sense. "I'll make certain of it. In the future, nae matter what, ye'll have this kenning, and can call on it."

She licked her lips. "Call on it?" she breathed.

He nodded firmly, his fingertips pressing into her chest, trying to make his certainty her own. "Tonight, I'll teach ye to love yerself, Treasure, and nae one can ever take that away from ye."

"That is…" She blinked, then exhaled. "That is exactly what I want."

Then that is exactly what she'd get.

Smiling crookedly, Cam relaxed, his fingers shifting slightly, until they found her prim buttons. "Then shall we begin?"

CHAPTER 2

THE SCOT MADE UNDRESSING a woman an art.

That was Jade's conclusion, as she realized her prim, businesslike blouse was somehow hanging open about her shoulders. When had that happened? Somewhere between his kisses and caresses, presumably, and she didn't care one bit.

At one point, she realized she'd dropped her empty glass and was all but straddling the man's lap as his lips worked on her neck, his fingers easily slipping her buttons from their moorings. And a part of her thought *You should be mortified.*

She should. She really should.

And she likely *would*.

After...

Because right now... Right now, she couldn't think, couldn't reason, couldn't doubt her plan. All she could do was *feel*. And *ai-ya*, but this man's lips, his hands, *felt* more incredible than anything she could've imagined before.

A Harlot's Guide had mentioned pleasure, but not this all-consuming pulse which threatened to overwhelm her. It was all she could do to remember to breathe!

His teeth nipped at her throat, his deft fingers already working on her corset.

She was about to give this nameless stranger her virginity, and although she *should* be ashamed at that thought, all she knew now was an eagerness.

As his lips worked along her shoulder, Jade dropped her head back with an encouraging moan, her hands reaching for his upper arms. Dear Lord, his arms were as hard as the rest of him. She ran her hands down them until they reached his forearms, which were revealed as the banyan fell back. She flexed her fingers outward, allowing his coarse hairs to rub against her palms, and his movements slowed.

"Too fast, Treasure?" he murmured against her shoulder.

She didn't have to think about it. "Too slow."

He smiled and, placing a quick kiss on her skin, turned his attention to his fingers' task.

She was breathless with anticipation by the time he peeled her blouse and corset from her. Now she sat on his lap in only her chemise and skirt, as he turned his attention to her boots. Of course, this required him bending, and Jade found it the most natural position in the world to grip his shoulders, then pull his head closer.

As his cheek settled against her breasts, she thought he made a little sound of satisfaction, and that—along with the hardness still pressed against her hip—told her he was enjoying this encounter as much as she.

The realization made her feel bold. Desirable.

This was the right decision.

Tomorrow, next week, next year, she might have to defend it. But now she knew she'd never have to defend this decision to *herself*, because this was exactly what she needed.

His large hands closed around her waist and lifted her. Sucking in a breath, she steadied herself on his shoulders until they were both standing, and then he was unclasping her skirt.

When she felt the heavy material sag around her knees, he stepped back.

She was left alone, confused. For lack of something else to do, she wriggled her hips until her skirt fell to the ground, and stepped out of it.

Still, he said nothing, and she forced herself to really look at him.

He was studying her. Not judgmentally, but with a look of…awe?

Suddenly self-conscious, Jade made to cover her bare arms, but he stopped her.

"Nay, lass," he whispered, reaching for her hand.

And when he led her toward the bed, all she could do was follow. Her stomach felt jumbled, the way it did before a bout, but this was…something else. Something anticipatory, special. The bed was beautiful, looming too large, covered in more pillows than anyone could use.

He led her past it.

To the little sitting area, and the large mirror.

Confused, she twisted her neck to keep the bed in her focus. Surely that was the natural progression of the evening?

Step One: Unbelievably arousing kisses.

Step Two: Removal of clothing.

Step Three: Passionate lovemaking atop that bed.

Although they'd likely have to remove some of the extraneous pillows. She could imagine getting lost among them.

But then he tugged her toward the large mirror, and she dragged her attention from the bed. Although she'd spent years in control—of herself and her father's empire—tonight she was learning to follow. To follow *him*.

And interestingly, she trusted him, this nameless stranger who made her want things she'd never before understood.

"Here," he murmured, settling her in front of the mirror,

his hands on her shoulders as he stood behind her. "What do ye see?"

Was this a game? Part of the seduction? Jade frowned as she glanced at herself in the mirror, her eyes instinctively flowing past her features to his.

He held her gaze in the glass. "Well?"

"I see me."

"Nay, ye dinnae." His lips twitched wryly. "Ye're looking at me."

Rolling her eyes slightly, she lifted a hand to her hip and cocked her brow at him. "You are saying you're *not* worthy of being looked at?"

His grin grew. "I'm imminently admirable, and devilishly handsome." He was. "But ye've looked at me long enough, lass. Look at *yerself.*"

With another little huff of exasperation—why wouldn't the man just get on with the lovemaking? Her body was already humming with need, thanks to him!—Jade turned her attention back to her own features in the mirror.

She looked...just as she always looked in a chemise. Skinny, tall. A little awkward, without her armor against the outside world.

He leaned in, his breath tickling her ear. "Look closer."

Squinting, she tried to see what he was talking about.

Lanky limbs, legs encased in stockings. Her black hair, which she'd inherited from her mother, was beginning to fall from its careful bun, thanks to his touches. She wore no cosmetics, but the changeable colors of her eyes—unusual in those with Chinese blood, her mother told her—seemed brighter somehow. Perhaps a result of what he'd done to her.

Her tongue darted out across her lower lip, and her thighs instinctively pressed together, trying to assuage the ache he'd raised in her core. Just through his *kisses.*

Under her thin chemise, Jade felt her nipples tighten, and

her gaze dropped to them to discover they *were* visible through the linen. Her breasts were heaving, and it took a dazed moment to realize it was because she was breathing heavily. She peeked lower, wondering if her arousal was visible any other way.

"Aye," he chuckled softly in her ear, and her gaze snapped back up to his in the mirror. "That is how I meant."

"What—"" She couldn't seem to form words.

He shifted closer, his hands still on her shoulders, his gaze still holding hers, until she could feel the long length of his hardness pressed against the cleft of her rear end. Instinctively, she flexed back against him, cradling him, aching for him.

"This treasure," he whispered, his hands skimming slowly down her arms. "This is what I see when I look at ye."

Her gaze switched back to herself in the mirror, just in time to see him shift his hold to her chemise, and lift it over her head in one swift move.

When she fought her way free of the linen, it was to see her reflection, nude except for her stockings. And she forgot how to breathe.

He reached for her hair, plucking the pins from her coiffure one by one. It was half-collapsed anyhow, and it took him no time at all before he was slipping her pins into the pocket of the banyan he was still wearing. Then, almost reverently, he ran both sets of fingers through her tresses, pulling them away from her neck, letting them fall forward around her face and shoulders.

"Beauty," he murmured as her eyes followed every move his hands made. "This is what I see."

His hands went back to her arms. "This power. This strength." His touch moved to her elbows, her forearms, as he pulled them away from her sides, displaying her before both of their gazes in the mirror.

"This is confidence, Treasure," he murmured, stepping forward once more so she could feel his arousal pressing against her. His hands skimmed up her sides until he cupped her breasts and she sucked in a dizzying gasp. "This is assurance. Ye are beautiful. Ye are magnificent."

She couldn't seem to tear her gaze away from his hands on her skin. She'd always known she had small breasts—it was what allowed her access to the sporting club, after all—but seeing them cupped so softly in such large hands...

She swallowed.

And then his thumb and forefinger found her nipples, rolling them each gently as she watched.

Her knees buckled, and she fell back against him.

When he huffed a little laugh, her gaze flew to his, but his attention was on his hands as well, that look of rapt *awe* back on his face.

Dimly, through her all-consuming *need*, she wondered how many times he'd done this. How many women he'd said these words to, how many women he'd touched like this. She was just one of many, to him, but to her...

This was special.

She swallowed, her hands falling to his forearms to support herself. He was tugging at her nipples now, the gentle caress seemingly tied directly to her core. Even without stroking herself, she could feel how wet she was, how ready.

Ready for what?

A Harlot's Guide had plenty of suggestions, and for the first time, Jade was going to experience at least one of them.

Her breaths were coming shorter, harsher, and he nudged her hair out of the way with his chin and began to drop kisses to her shoulder. One of his hands left her breast and slid down her belly. She was still holding his forearm, but somehow, he reversed their positions...

And when their linked fingers reached her wispy curls at

the junction of her thighs, *hers* were the ones to touch her arousal first.

"Do ye feel that, lass?" he murmured, his lips finding that sensitive spot beneath her ear. "Do ye feel how wet ye are? Wet for me, wet with *need*."

He pressed her fingers through her curls, and she made a vague sound of approval, agreement. *Hunger.*

"Aye, my Treasure. Ye feel it?"

"Yes," she managed to whimper, her eyes fluttering closed, as if that would help hide her from the sensations which threatened to overwhelm her.

"Good."

The only warning she received was when his hand dropped away from her wetness. Her eyes flashed open in time to see him stepping away from her, his hand closing around her wrist.

She stumbled when he pulled her gently backward, and he caught her. Instead of helping her upright, though, he settled her in one of the wing-backed chairs, with the plush arms and seat.

As she sat, he lifted—both her and the chair—and it wasn't until he'd placed it in front of the mirror that she processed the strength that must have required. But she didn't have time to consider it, because he caught her attention again when he dropped his hands to the chair's arms—standing between her and the mirror—and leaned in.

She was close enough to see the circle of dark blue around the rims of his irises...close enough to feel his breath on her forehead. Close enough to kiss him.

He grinned. "Ye've come to learn about pleasure. To lose yer virginity on yer own terms. Right, Treasure?"

Why was he still calling her that? Confused, she nodded.

With a curt nod of his own, he straightened. "And ye trust me?"

"I...shouldn't."

His grin flashed. "I ken that, but ye do, aye? I swear I'll make this a memorable night for ye."

She swallowed and rested her head back, one set of fingers trailing unbidden along the bare skin of her stomach, trying to recapture the sensation of his touch. "You already have," she whispered.

"Aye," he murmured, as he whirled about and stalked toward an armoire. She didn't have to twist her head to see him open the top drawer and pull something out, because she could see him in the tall mirror.

The tall mirror in front of which she sat, all her bare skin on display.

She studied herself, trying to see what he had seen. Strength. Power. Confidence. He'd seen that in her, and he didn't even know her.

Her other hand rose to join the first, and she watched them —watched herself as if apart, somehow—cup her breasts, roll the nipples between her fingers, the way he'd done. The sensation wasn't quite the same, but the ache between her thighs intensified, and she allowed her stocking-clad legs to fall open, until she was staring at the very heart of her.

Aching. Dripping. *Needing.*

It felt so wrong, to be watching herself like this, but... He was right. It *was* empowering.

And then her vision of that most intimate part of her was obscured—by him. The Scot leaned over her again, closer, his lips claiming hers. His kiss was hard and fast and desperate, and left her panting as he pulled away.

She didn't have time to understand what had happened, before he'd planted his hands on the arms of the chair and was kissing his way down her body. "I'm glad to see ye were busy without me," he murmured in between kisses.

And then his lips captured her nipple, and she jerked

upright. But as he worried it gently between his teeth, she exhaled, relaxing into a puddle of desire, and he huffed quietly in laughter.

One of his hands found her core, his fingers sliding easily along her wet cleft, settling against the bud of her pleasure, which she'd occasionally examined herself.

As he switched his ministrations to her other nipple, she realized he'd done quite a lot of examining himself.

Once more, her eyes met her own gaze in the mirror, over his banyan-clad bent back and blond curls. Was that really her? Miss Jade Thacker, allowing some stranger to sup at her breasts and fondle her clitoris? The thoughts were vague, disjointed, distracted by the pleasure he was bringing her body.

Almost in a trance, she lifted her fingers to twine through his curls, and was rewarded by a grunt of approval from him, which reminded her of the sound he'd made earlier when she'd cradled him against her.

But before she had a chance to try that again, he was moving down her body, settling on his knees between her thighs. Without looking up, without ceasing his gentle strokes, The Scot lowered his mouth to her core.

Oh.

Oh, hell.

Oh, heaven.

In the mirror, Jade saw her eyes go wide, but her entire attention was on the way this man's mouth made her feel.

Slowly, she eased back against the chair, her fingers digging into his scalp, trying to hold him in place. Jade allowed her eyes to flutter shut, too overwhelmed by what he was doing to her to have to worry about *seeing* as well.

She felt his tongue drag along her cleft, before settling over the bud of her pleasure, teasing it with his tongue and then teeth. One of his fingers slid along her wetness, the way hers did when she needed release…but it didn't feel anything like *that*.

His hands were large and capable, and she instinctively opened her legs to allow him more space. He made a sound of approval, but didn't look up.

But that hum… That hum of appreciation was more than she could stand. Whether it was the fluttery sensation in her stomach at the thought of his approval, or the vibrations against her most intimate part…

Jade moaned as she felt her orgasm finally—*finally*—burst upon her. Her rear end arched off the chair, her heels taking her weight as she pushed herself upward, against his lips. He hummed again, and *ai-ya!* She couldn't breathe.

But the way her core pulsed wasn't enough. Moaning low in her throat, she pushed higher, closer to him, needing… needing *something.*

His gentle ministrations eased, as her pulsing pleasure did. It wasn't until she opened her eyes that she'd realized she'd closed them. She was slumped back against the chair, chest heaving, and he was staring up at her.

From here, she could see the evidence of her arousal in the shininess around his lips and chin, her wetness clinging to his faint stubble making him look far more wonderful than he should.

He smiled.

She frowned. "Was that it?"

His laugh was a rumble, little more than a chuckle, and his alluring eyes crinkled at the corners as he held her gaze. *Ai-ya*, the man was handsome enough, desirable enough, to make an angel weep!

"Not enough for you, Treasure?"

She was flustered by her response to him, and her body— her core, still open and displayed to him—was still pulsing with desire which hadn't diminished. That was the only reason she shook her head at the same time saying, "I could have done this myself."

His laughter increased. "*All* by yourself?"

When he dragged his tongue across his upper lip, making a show of tasting her desire, she found herself breathless once more.

"That's what I thought," he murmured. He shifted his weight, and she wondered if he was comfortable kneeling at her feet. "Well, let us continue."

It wasn't until he lowered his face toward her curls that she realized what he meant, and she tightened her fingers in his hair to stop him.

He froze, blue flashing up toward her. "No?"

"I…" She shook her head, fighting the urge to press her thighs closed, trapping him between them. "I thought I was here for sex."

"Ye're here to lose yer virginity on yer terms," he reminded her. "Now, ye'll have to trust me to do this correctly."

Trust him? She didn't *know* him. And yet…

She exhaled, loosening her hold on him as her knees fell apart once more.

This time…well, there *wasn't* a time. It seemed to her as if time was standing still, each of his licks, suckles, caresses taking place at the same moment, and yet drawn out over the course of several years. Her heartbeat pumped in time to his murmurs, praises, hums, as she alternated between watching him, watching herself in the mirror, and allowing her eyes to close so she could just *feel*.

This time, he touched her *everywhere*. His lips traced parts of her body she'd never considered baring to another human, much less a stranger still partially dressed. And through it all, the beat of hunger, of *need* grew steadily harsher and more demanding.

It was as if, now that her body had felt pleasure once, it was unwilling to settle for anything less.

And then…he sat back on his heels, his hand still spread across her curls, his thumb still maddeningly teasing her pearl, the heel of his palm pressed where she needed the pressure the most. But she wanted more. She wanted him *inside* her.

"Ye're close, Treasure."

"I'm ready," she gasped.

He nodded, and stood. As her eyes followed him upward, she saw his robe had become untied, the beautiful blue silk opening to reveal his untucked shirt and trousers tented by his obvious desire. Unconsciously, she licked her lips, her gaze fastened on that bulge, knowing it would soon be inside her.

But instead of reaching for that bulge, he thrust his hand into the pocket of his banyan, and emerged holding…something long and smooth and tapered. A phallus.

Her gaze landed on it in confusion.

"Do ye ken what this is?"

It looked like… Her gaze slammed back to his, but there was no mocking or teasing in his eyes.

"The French call this *godemichet*, and there are plenty here who ken it as a dildo. A replacement for an erect cock."

He was being so…matter-of-fact about it. She swallowed, her fingers itching to feel it, but battered by confusion.

He seemed to sense it, and reached down to take her hand. He wrapped it around the smooth object, and she identified it as being made of ivory. But then he was guiding her hand—and it—to her weeping entrance.

She tensed, knowing what would happen, but…he released her, straightening, stepping to the side. Her hand—and the dildo—poised at her core, she followed his movements in the mirror.

He pulled the other chair closer to her— No, not to her. He pulled it toward the mirror, settling the chair beside hers, and a little behind. She watched in confusion, frozen, every inch of her body attuned to his movements and the pleasure he'd brought her.

Until he settled into the chair, his gaze finding hers in the mirror.

"I don't understand," she breathed.

"Aye, Treasure, I think ye do." His grin wasn't wry this time, but gentle.

When he slid his penis—nay, his *cock*, he'd called it—from his trousers, her lips parted in a silent exclamation.

It was so close to her. If she reached out, she might be able to touch it, as he sat so near. But instead, she stared at it—at him—in the mirror. The mirror made it more bearable, less overwhelming.

Then, his movement casual, he began to stroke himself. "Look what ye've done to me, lass," he murmured in that low baritone, the one which wrapped around her heart and pulled. "I'm so hard, so ready, and it's all because of ye."

Her hand, the one holding the dildo at her weeping entrance, began to tremble.

"Ye need this," he spoke again, his words measured and calm, as calm as his strokes. "Ye need something hard inside ye. Something like *this*, aye?"

She whimpered, her gaze still on his cock.

"Do it," he whispered. "Claim yerself."

She could no more refrain from following his order than she could order her heart to cease beating.

Nostrils flaring with her inhale, she pushed the dildo inside of her. Miss Jade Thatcher took her own virginity.

She whimpered as the device stretched her, but it was nothing compared to the groan of satisfaction he made, accompanying a heavy sigh, as if he hadn't been certain she'd do it.

Unmoving, trying to adjust to the sensation of something

inside her, Jade watched his strokes increase in pace, becoming more frantic.

And...she remembered she didn't know this man. She wouldn't know him tomorrow, or next year, but she *would* know herself.

Her free hand dropped to her breast, and she pinched her nipple the way he'd taught her to.

"Aye," he gasped, his breath hitching, his gaze fastened to the place where the dildo disappeared inside her. "Like that."

It was his approval which broke through her hesitation, more than anything else. He'd done so much for her, and she realized she could do something for him.

Feeling bold now, she lifted one leg, shifted, and draped it across the armrest nearest to him. She was splayed open now, and from his hungry gaze in the mirror, he couldn't get enough of it.

Tentatively, she pushed the dildo in just a bit farther, and was rewarded twice; once by his groan of approval, and once by the sudden sharp bite of pleasure which sparked through her. It was a different feeling than the one which had consumed her earlier, but...*better* somehow.

This time, she pulled the smoothness from her an inch or two, before pushing it slowly back in, and in the mirror, his eyes flashed in hunger. Emboldened by his obvious approval, she did it again, nearly whimpering from her own satisfaction.

It wasn't long before she found her rhythm. Her thrusts weren't as energetic as his strokes, but each one sent a bolt of bliss through her, especially after she dropped her hand to her clitoris, trying to mimic the movement of his tongue with her fingers.

"Jesus Christ, lass, do ye have any idea how—" He bit off the blasphemy with a groan as she brought her finger to her lips, intrigued by the salty-sweetness.

They sat, splayed open for each other's amusement, staring

openly through the mirror, each heartbeat matching the other. She was panting, and his lips were open greedily as he followed the movements of her hands.

"Come for me, lass," he rasped. When she met his eyes in the mirror, he nodded. "Come for me, now."

She wasn't used to being commanded, but at that moment, she realized what she'd been missing. At the harshness of his words, Jade sucked in a gasp, and felt her inner core tightening around the smooth dildo.

And then he groaned and dropped back against the chair, his gaze flashing to hers in the glass as *something* erupted around the top of his pumping hand.

With a groan, she pressed the base of her hand against her pelvis, providing the pressure she was desperate for, as she slid the dildo in and out at a greater speed.

Ai-ya, but this was… This was…

With a wordless keen, Jade fell over the edge and into the abyss.

It was much later—or possibly all too soon—when she came back to herself, chest heaving, to find him kneeling before her again. She ignored the wanton in the mirror, and instead focused on him. When had he cleaned up and tucked himself back in?

In bemusement, she watched him gently slip the device from her core, placing it to one side as he cleaned her with a warm cloth. Then he shifted forward and slipped one arm around her, pulling her toward him and upright.

Before she could understand, she was standing, and he was…he was pulling the blue robe from his shoulders and slipping it around hers. The silk felt decadent against her bare skin, which tingled from its recent pleasure.

He led her to the bed—finally!—and pulled down the counterpane before urging her to climb in. He joined her, and once there, pulled her into his arms, tucking her head under his chin and settling back against the too-many pillows with every impression of relaxation.

And it *was* relaxing. Her body still hummed, and her thighs felt tight, but not for long. His heart beat steadily beside her ear as she slowly allowed herself to just...*be*. No thinking about the future, no thinking about what just happened. Just...be.

After a long while—long enough for Jade to assume he'd fallen asleep, The Scot rumbled softly, "I trust ye'll remember tonight's lesson, Treasure?"

She was tired. Tired and sated and boneless. But even so, she roused herself to answer him. "That I am powerful." She'd taken her *own* virginity, with his help.

"Aye," he chuckled, and she felt it throughout her chest. "Ye are. And beautiful, and worthy. Ye can do anything ye wish."

"Aye," she mimicked, then interrupted herself with a yawn.

He huffed again, which might've been a laugh, as he began stroking her hair.

It was too alluring to resist.

For this moment, she was safe. Safe and confident and beautiful. The Scot—a surprisingly thoughtful stranger—was caring for her, and she...she could relax.

A smile tugged at her lips, and Jade fell asleep in his arms.

CHAPTER 3

"Ye call that an attack?" Cam scoffed affably at his opponent, whose lunge had been easy to knock aside.

The arrogantly infuriating Baron Buthert scowled behind his wire mask, and darted forward once more, this attack causing Cam to step back as he parried.

"I call that a feint," growled Buthert. "*This* is an attack."

Cam was grinning as he met each of his opponent's moves with his own, his focus on the tip of Buthert's foil, knowing that—since this match wasn't official, and wasn't being scored—it was up to him to record the hits against him.

Luckily, he was a better fencer than this blowhard.

He'd met Buthert once or twice on the strip here at the London Fencing Club, and each time, Cam had been unimpressed. The baron—what was his name? Something regal. Not *regal* regal, like Reginald, but regal as in named-after-one-of-those-useless-English-kings. George? Edward? Whatever his name was, Buthert fenced like a man who'd learned it at school because that was considered *the* thing to do.

In other words, not *nearly* as good as Cam, who'd become

very, very good at working out his irritation and insignificance here against men who thought themselves far superior.

"Damn!" Buthert fell back, breathing heavily, after Cam's foil swept through his defenses and bent against the man's canvas-covered chest. "A point."

Good-naturedly, Cam saluted. "Again?"

"Of course, again," growled Buthert, settling into the *en garde* position. "It was a lucky blow!"

Cam hid his grin as he easily blocked his tiring opponent's lunges. *A lucky blow?* Buthert was one of those lordlings who thought themselves so much better than men like Cam, just because of blood. They often failed to remember that Cam shared the same blood they did; only his parents hadn't been married.

Aye, he was a bastard, which allowed entitled men like Buthert to sneer down their noses at him. But Cam's father was a powerful Highland laird, and his mother the daughter of an earl, even if he had been born out of wedlock. He'd been afforded all the best when it came to education.

As long as ye played the part they expected from ye.

Grimly, he knocked aside that thought as easily as he knocked aside Buthert's blows. Neither of his families had wanted him, but they'd supported him financially at least. And he'd built himself a new family at school; brothers, fellow bastards who were now his closest friends.

Besides, he was far from destitute. His investments had more than paid off, which allowed him the chance to visit the club twice weekly and keep his skills honed. And while his stepfather might want nothing to do with him, the MacKays liked him well enough.

Too bad they lived so far from civilization.

Blast! While he'd been distracted, Buthert had managed to land a blow, and now crowed mockingly about it as he returned to his place.

Cam was perfectly happy to be seen as the affable layabout charmer the rest of Society had deemed him; the rake, the playboy. Whatever his personal feelings about Buthert, it was infinitely easier to salute him obligingly and call out, "A point!"

"My lord," the toad corrected.

Cam pretended not to understand as he settled into guard position. "Hmm?" His back hand rose elegantly.

"A point, *my lord*," Buthert elaborated, as if Cam were an idiot.

"What's that, Buthert?" Cam asked as he launched a sudden attack. "I couldnae quite hear ye. The mask, ye ken."

And then both men were silent, save for the grunts as they blocked and lunged. Buthert was tiring, and Cam decided to finish the match.

With a flurry of movements, foils clanged noisily together, the sound a sort of music. Buthert fell back, panting.

"Good Lord, you barbarian! Are you trying to kill me?"

Easily, Cam shrugged. "Shelbourne and Northwich were both otherwise engaged today, and I needed a good workout."

"Northwich has never been beaten," Buthert blustered, as he stepped back, his blade raised to indicate a break.

Happy to oblige him, Cam saluted as well. "Aye, at blades or rock throwing or the long jump, or whatever barbaric pastimes an athlete like him gets up to. Thank fook he's married now and has found other ways to deplete his energy."

"I cannot believe you expect me to speculate on the man's energy." Buthert sounded vaguely disgusted as he pulled his mask from his face and shook his head as he tucked his foil under his arm. Lips curled, he stepped off the fencing strip and headed toward the sidelines, where a servant waited with beverages.

Cam tucked his foil under the arm holding his mask, and ran his gloved hand through his hair as he followed. The

London Fencing Club was considered the city's premiere sporting establishment, but Cam was only interested in the fencing strips. On days like today—when he was feeling antsy and full of coiled energy—he could always find a match.

In fact, the little concierge had brightened when he saw Cam enter, and had tittered happily. "I have a new opponent for you, Mr. MacKay! Soon!"

Cam had nodded his approval, and gone to find a match while he waited for the mystery opponent. Buthert had barely been a warm-up.

Now, Cam placed his sword and mask on the table, and carefully pulled his right glove from his hand. He'd had the thing specially made, at great expense. It matched his jacket, of course.

"Red," Buthert said with a disparaging sigh as he lifted his water. Apparently he was bored, to still be standing here conversing with Cam. "You always do care to make a scene, but red leather?"

"Excuse me, this is *scarlet*," Cam corrected haughtily, peering down at himself as he slapped his glove against his opposite palm, then reached for his own refreshment. The staff here knew his preference for sweets, and had mixed juice and water for him. "And ye cannae expect me to be seen in public looking anything less than *remarkable*."

Although the new trend was for jackets and trousers to be all white or black—or sometimes even a combination—Cam was never one for dullness when *scarlet* was an option.

Buthert, however, wasn't impressed. "It's practically choking you. How can you breathe in that thing?"

Touching the high collar, Cam felt one side of his lips tug upward. "Easily. And I need to protect my throat, aye? Ye think I'm likely to do it with that pedestrian nonsense the rest of ye use?" He nodded mockingly at the other man's standard canvas jacket. "Ye're no' even wearing a belt."

"That's because I expect you to be able to find my midline without the need for visual aids." Buthert cocked an eyebrow at Cam's wide black belt, which indicated the line below which an opponent's hits didn't score.

Cam flexed his fingers and rolled his shoulders. "Aye, but ye're less experienced than I, so I had to give ye a target."

Buthert's nostrils flared at the lighthearted insult, and his knuckles tightened around his glass. Frankly, Cam was surprised the man was still standing here, and hadn't made an effort to retreat to an easier match, or the lockers.

"Should we find ye a training master's plastron?" he sneered. "Perhaps Master Beltrande has a spare one for you. One with a big red heart painted over the chest, so I know where to aim?"

Instead of rising to the bait, Cam affected innocence. "Och, aye? Do ye think ye might need a target so large? Few of yer hits actually resulted in points, ye ken."

Buthert scowled "That's because your jacket blinded me. It's garish."

How like the man to make excuses. "It's stylish," Cam defended.

The dark-haired lord curled his lips as he looked Cam up and down. "And you're not wearing shoes."

Nodding, Cam handed the empty glass to a servant and began to pull his glove back on. "Because it wasn't a real match. I prefer to fight barefoot; it improves my balance."

"You look like an idiot," Buthert grumbled.

Cam couldn't help it; he burst into chuckles at the other man's pouting. "Ye're just indignant ye were beaten so soundly by a man without shoes."

The other man opened his mouth—likely to fire an insult back, but they were interrupted by the concierge, who bustled up with a beaming grin.

"The Chinaman has agreed to spar with you, Mr. MacKay.

I told of your prowess, and he'll meet you on strip number three in five minutes."

Before Cam could do more than nod in agreement, the little man bustled off again. Buthert watched him go, and *harumphed* under his breath.

"*Prowess*? And why in damnation would a *Chinaman* be allowed into my club?"

Shrugging, Cam reached for his mask, brushing off the other man's ignorance. "He must be a member, to spar here. But it is odd, I'll grant that. Ye understand I'm curious, and must leave ye."

Buthert waved magnanimously, as if a king granting a favor. Cam hid his grimace as he pulled his mask down over his face, saying a silent prayer the other man would find someone else to bother and wouldn't stand here to watch Cam's match with the Chinaman.

Whoever he was.

He padded barefoot to the six-foot-wide fencing strip, then bounced a few times and rolled his shoulders to prepare himself. Anyone who knew him as the languid, flirtatious beast who prowled the ballroom floors, secure in his welcome as the illegitimate son of a Highland laird and the Baroness Codpeas, would hardly recognize him here. When it came to fencing, he was focused and sure of his ability.

But there was something...*off* today. Something had been off for the last few days, and Cam didn't like it. He felt hollow, unfulfilled, and although the bouts with Buthert had helped, Cam still felt jittery, deep in his chest.

Unfulfilled, eh?

Aye, it had started the night of his last assignation. The woman who'd come to his hotel room to lose her virginity on her own terms, and had come apart with his tongue on her. She'd done exactly what she hadn't known she'd needed; she'd taken control of her own carnal appetite, and made it work for her.

God Almighty, just the memory of her pinching her own nipples as she slid that bone-white dildo in and out of her black curls... Well, the middle of the London Fencing Club was no place for a cockstand, he had to remind himself.

Besides, it would *completely* ruin the line of these trousers.

He rolled his shoulders again, and forced a few sharp breaths in and out before holding one for the count of five, and exhaling even more slowly. It was an old trick Jean Beltrande had taught him, as Cam's mother had hired the fencing master to tutor her sons.

She might have been seduced by the charming and gregarious Argus MacKay in her youth, but as the daughter of a sought-after earl, she'd still managed a marriage with some benefits...including further children, and fencing masters.

Unsurprisingly, thinking of Beltrande and his mother had done wonders for Cam's inconvenient cockstand.

Huzzah! Now he wouldn't need to worry about crushing the poor bastard between his thighs as he sparred.

Speaking of which...

The concierge bobbed his little head like a chicken as he escorted Cam's new opponent toward the strip. Unusually, the other man already had his wire mesh mask firmly in place, so it was impossible to get a look at him. He was slightly built, and taller than the concierge but shorter than Cam, and carried himself with a swagger which suggested he was bluffing.

He wore no gloves, and Cam's gaze lingered in interest on the man's lithe hand, which already gripped the handle of his foil.

Well, if he wanted to risk his knuckles and trust only in the sword's guard, then it was up to him. Cam allowed every man some peculiarities. Gloveless opponent versus shoeless opponent.

At least the Chinaman was wearing soft leather indoor shoes—the toe of the right foot extended almost a full inch, for balance, the way Stroke's did. And he wore a high-collared white canvas, the same as Stroke, which buttoned up the left side. This, as well as the shoe on his leading foot, told Cam his opponent was right-handed.

With the man's mask fully in place, Cam didn't bother lifting his for the traditional greeting. Instead, he nodded affably as he swung his sword back and forth to limber his right arm.

"Chinaman, eh? Are ye any good with that foil?"

Instead of replying the smaller man dropped his chin in an arrogant nod, which made Cam smile behind his mask.

"We shall see, laddie."

His opponent offered a silent salute, then dropped easily to an *en garde* position, his back hand held outward, not in the French style, but with a flair all his own.

Oh, this would be *fun.*

His challenger was the first to lunge into a lightning-fast attack which might've startled another man. Cam suspected the Chinaman was used to being smaller than his opponents, and was using that to his advantage.

Or rather, would *try* to use that to his advantage, because although he was bigger, Cam was just as light on his feet as the other man.

The pair of them danced back and forth, feinting and thrusting and parrying, each trying to get a feel of the other man's style. And Cam was, in spite of himself, impressed.

It had been a while since he'd sparred with Northwich, or any other fencer this nimble and skilled. The Chinaman had a style Cam couldn't quite recognize; it was obvious he hadn't learned from Master Beltrande, or any other French tutor.

But interestingly, the differences in the other man's style made Cam feel...well, not exactly at ease, but more relaxed. The jittery feeling he'd been experiencing over the last days slowly dissipated, and his lips curled upward. He didn't have time for introspection, but it was impossible to deny that for the first time since he'd woken to find his new Treasure gone, he felt calmer.

Likely because ye're matched with a man who kens what he's doing, eh?

Fencing with the Chinaman *was* more fun than sparring with Stroke.

Cam always felt most free when he could allow his mind to wander, only part of it focused on the next attack, the next block, while allowing his arms and hips and feet to do the real work. The ability didn't diminish today; he scored the first point, his opponent the second, and the third was Cam's again.

In fact, although their styles were very different, they were well-matched, trading points evenly. Once, after losing a hit to the smaller man, Cam retreated and saluted with a wry grin. "Ye *are* good. Are ye really Chinese?"

This time, the smaller man's *en garde* faltered. "Are you Scottish?" he finally growled in a gravelly sort of tone. It was clear he was trying to disguise his voice, and Cam assumed it was because he was younger than the average member of the club. A lad would do his best to appear older, would he not?

Cam gave a mocking salute. "I am." *The Scot*, they called him around London.

Or rather, it was what the ladies called him. A very certain kind of lady.

A lady like yer Treasure, aye?

He hadn't *meant* to fall asleep holding her. It had been a first for him, honestly. He routinely met ladies at The Savoy, seducing them with careful touches, champagne, and things to nibble on: oysters, artichokes, chocolate, bare skin. The oysters usually worked wonders.

But his Treasure had been...different. He'd known from the moment he'd seen her that it would be a special evening, and it was. God Almighty, he would've given his eye teeth to have been inside her when she burst into pleasure, but he had made a vow long ago, and held true to it.

But seeing *her* bring herself to completion, and knowing it was what she'd needed...? There'd been something almost reverent to it. Mythical, religious, *spiritual*.

And not just because he'd orgasmed at the same time.

Although that had helped, certainly.

She'd fallen asleep in his arms. He shouldn't have liked that as much as he had, and Cam had found his own eyes closing as well.

Whereas normally, his well-sated clients left him with kisses and fond farewells and plans for future assignations, this time, he'd...tucked himself into the bed, holding her. And they'd slept.

When he'd woken, he'd been surprised by quite a few things:

The fact he'd slept better than he had in a long while.

The fact he was fully dressed, when he preferred to sleep in the nude.

The fact he was still in a hotel room.

The fact the uneaten oysters he'd had delivered the night before were becoming a bit aromatic.

The fact *she was gone*.

He'd found a wallet, containing his usual fee, sitting beside the dildo she'd used the night before. Both were placed beside his copy of *A Harlot's Guide* on the chair where she'd hooked one leg over the arm so he could see her core as she'd fooked herself, prominently reflected in that beautiful, damnable mirror.

Cam had taken the long route home, and dropped the entire wallet in the collection box in front of the Holy Sisters of Perpetual Snarks' Saving Grace and the Rest of Them as Well charity orphanage.

He didn't know who she was, he didn't know if he'd ever see her again. What they'd shared that night had been because she was about to belong to another man. But even if she'd never know of his charity, there was no way he would take money for what they'd shared.

Hell, he'd likely *pay* for the opportunity to see her again.

The Chinaman's foil bent almost double against scarlet canvas as the smaller man lunged past Cam's guard and stabbed him in the chest.

"Fook me!" Cam blurted, stumbling backward, an incredulous laugh escaping his lips. "That one ought to count double!"

From his place by the refreshments, Buthert called out mockingly, "You were distracted!"

Cam watched his opponent's head turn briefly toward the spoiled arse, then the impassive mask dipped once in acknowledgement of Buthert's assessment, and Cam had to smile again.

"I cannae fight both ye *and* distraction at once." He lifted his weapon to guard again. "So I will focus more closely on you, sir."

The smaller man nodded once more.

Talkative fellow, eh?

It was Cam's turn to attack, and his opponent turned aside his lunge. Again they fell into an easy back-and-forth, the clang of the foils as they beat against each other almost musical. Points were traded, quips were made—entirely by Cam, of course—and their breathing grew heavier.

Reveling in the stretch and pull of his muscles, Cam found himself smiling, even as sweat tangled the curls at his forehead. He hadn't had a workout like this in a while, and his opponent was still going.

However, it was becoming obvious the smaller man's strength was flagging.

When Cam scored his fourth point in a row—a hit his opponent should've easily been able to parry, had the man been fresh and attentive, Cam held up a gloved hand. "Had enough?"

His only answer was a sharp shake of the other man's head, as he settled once more into guard position. Cam, who admired tenacity, shrugged and chuckled.

He could feel the other man watching for an opening, his movements more conservative than even minutes before. Preserving his strength, possibly?

Even as Cam had the thought, his opponent burst into a flurry of lunges, which completely caught him off guard. Cam was able to parry the first wild swing, but the second caught him low on his side; a hit.

Scowling, he stepped back, nodding in acknowledgment and blinking away sweat. "Good thing this match isn't being scored, aye? That was an illegal swing."

His opponent didn't respond, other than to raise his foil once more.

His foil…aye, that was the issue; the man had put aside the steady lunge, thrust of the foil and had used more of a backsword's swing. "Would ye like to switch weapons?" he asked in a mocking tone of voice. "I'm certain the club has backswords we might use."

The smaller man shuffled back a half step, then forward again, in what might have been hesitation. He shook his head mutely.

Cam was sweaty and his good humor was fast evaporating. He lifted his foil, gave the barest minimum of salute, and attacked. His opponent parried twice, three times, then went on the attack himself.

Again, his lunge was a feint, a disguise for what turned into a wild swing more at home to a backsword or sabre than a foil. But Cam knocked away the attack, now that he knew what to look for.

"Yer switch might work for others, lad, but I've studied the *claidheamh*," he growled.

Without stopping to acknowledge his words, the smaller man swung to the left, then down. Cam raised his foil to parry...and his opponent switched styles as easily as breathing, turning his swing into a thrust and slipping easily past Cam's guard.

His foil jabbed against Cam's chest, surprising another burst of laughter from Cam.

"Och, well done, laddie." Cam laughed, reaching for his mask. "I concede."

He pulled the heavy wire mesh from his face and shook out his sweaty curls, still smiling. He turned to invite his opponent to join in for some cold, watered juice.

But when he did, the smaller man stumbled backward, his mask still hiding his features, in what seemed like surprise.

"Are ye aright?" Cam called, but the other man just shook his head frantically, his foil dangling forgotten from his hand.

Behind him, there was the sound of a throat clearing. Keeping half his attention on the body language of his opponent, Cam shifted to see one of the club's servants holding a silver salver with a letter atop it. Addressed to *him*.

Frowning, Cam tucked his foil under his arm and reached for the letter. "From my father?"

The servant maintained a blank expression. "Indeed, sir. Your butler thought it might be important, and had it sent here."

Lips curled ruefully, Cam shrugged. He'd been known to ignore his father's letters—usually nagging him about taking on more responsibility—for days if possible, and his butler knew him well enough to send it here, where Cam couldn't ignore it.

Humming thoughtfully, Cam stepped toward the refreshments, only to remember his recent bout. He glanced over his shoulder to invite his opponent to join him once more, and realized the man had disappeared.

Curious.

Cam made a note to ask the concierge for "the Chinaman's" name, so he might set up future matches, but most of his attention was on the letter in his hand. When he reached the table, it was to discover Buthert still there.

Damnation.

Still, Cam nodded politely and dropped his mask and foil on the table, before reaching for a glass of cold juice.

Buthert kept his tone neutral—although it was possible to hear the curiosity there—when he said, "That was quite the match. And ended by a mysterious letter. Are you going to open it?"

Finishing the last of the juice, Cam rolled the cold glass across his forehead. "It could be a private matter."

The other man snorted derisively. "I saw the postmark upon it. I am assuming your father is writing to scold you for spending his money on membership to such an elite club." Buthert pretended to study his fingernails. "And frankly, I would like that very much."

Instead of being offended, or threatening to hit the other man, Cam found himself amused at Buthert's so thinly disguised curiosity. Likely the lord was just bored, and wanted to know what kind of letter was important enough to interrupt a man's sport.

Well, since Cam himself was curious, he might as well

learn the answer. With a shrug, he slit open the envelope and skimmed the letter.

"Well, what does it say?" Buthert asked impatiently.

Cam cleared this throat before reading aloud, "Greetings, son, weather is fine, yer sisters are loud, *et cetera, et cetera.*"

"That's *it*? How boring."

Cam was barely paying attention. Because it *wasn't* like his father to send such an innocuous letter, especially one his butler thought it imperative Cam read.

His stomach feeling achingly hollow, Cam scanned his father's handwriting, the news and complaints as predictable as always. Which didn't explain why his hands had begun to shake.

He found what he was dreading in the fourth paragraph.

Now, for some words on marriage by proxy, Cameron.

You and I both ken you will not be my heir. Your younger brother will be the next Laird MacKay, and an earl to boot! But that does not mean you have nothing. There is so much potential in you, son. You have used it to woo and charm your way into Society's graces, which impresses me. But you ken I will not be completely impressed until you have made something of yourself. Something useful.

And grandbairns will not hurt, either.

To both of these ends, it is my pleasure to inform you of your recent marriage. I stood in for you, and your stepmother stood in for your new wife. She is a wonderful lass—your wife, not my Mary, whom you cannot have, being she is married to me and the mother of your brother and sisters. But your wife is my wife's niece, and her father left me in charge of her funds until she comes of age. She's a smart lass, good head for business, which should be the kick in the arse you need.

Jade is her name. Jade MacKay, now, and I'm proud to claim her as a daughter-in-law as well as a niece.

Congratulations on your marriage, son! I will meet you at The Cottage on the 18th of this month to pour a drink in your honor.

Or to listen to you moan and complain about what is already done, more likely.

Make me proud, lad!

Your Loving Father, et cetera and whatnot,
Laird Argus MacKay

CAM SUSPECTED MORE than just his hands were shaking as he crumpled the letter in his fist. Marriage by proxy?

Marriage in general?

Fooking married?

"So…" Buthert began breezily, clearly trying to portray the answer didn't matter one whit to him. "Anything interesting?"

"What day is it?" Cam knew his whisper was harsh, as he stared at the nonchalant letter which was going to ruin his life. Wasn't it already the fifteenth?

Buthert frowned "The fifteenth. Why?"

Instead of answering, Cam took a big gulp from another glass. *Married?* Perhaps the surprise was what caused him to ask, "Do ye ken anything about marriage by proxy?"

"Is that not what occurs when someone stands in for another at his wedding?" Buthert chortled, cruel mirth suddenly spilling across his face. "Do not say *you* have been married by proxy? Oh, this is delightful!" He went so far as to clap his hands together as he chuckled. "The Scottish bastard, caught in the marriage trap!"

Angry at himself for allowing this sniveling, spoiled

lordling to know his troubles, Cam growled, "This cannae be legal." Part of him wanted to rip up the letter, but then he wouldn't have anything to wave in Da's face when the man arrived at The Cottage. "No' even in Scotland."

But Buthert was still chuckling. "Scotland is barbaric, indeed. The marriage rules are quite backward, as I recall."

Backward? *Bah.*

Cam gathered up his mask and foil, his leather gloves tightening around the blade, the recent exercise forgotten. "You can damned well wager I'll be finding out all I can before I submit to this. And if I *am* married—to some cousin I've never met—I'll be sure to fight it!"

"Aye, that's the spirit." Buthert was clearly gleeful at Cam's misfortune, judging from his mocking tone. "Remember, no matter how the marriage took place, consummation is the key."

Horrified at the idea, Cam turned, wide-eyed. The dark-haired man was smirking when he explained, "Once your marriage is consummated, it cannot be annulled. And I, personally, am delighted to discover a rake such as you, placed in a situation where he would not want to charm his way under a lady's skirt."

Annulment.

Surprisingly, the reminder helped calm Cam, helped him ignore Buthert's mocking.

An annulment, aye. He would cling to that. No matter what nonsense Da had pulled, an annulment was still possible. All Cam had to do was keep his hands off his new "wife", until he could get the whole damned thing worked out.

But first, he was going to meet his father and find out just what in the *hell* the old man thought he was doing. Three days was more than enough time to pack and catch a train to the Lowlands, where Da would meet him at the small estate he'd gifted Cam years ago.

"Aye," he growled, his gaze already focused on the future and getting out of this mess. "I suspect it'll no' be a problem to keep my hands off whatever harpy my father's deemed capable of taking me in hand."

No consummating. Simple.

CHAPTER 4

OF ALL THE NERVE. Jade could recall a time, when paid for doing a certain job, men actually *went and did the bloody job*! A fare from the train station in the village to the adorably named The Cottage should've meant delivering her to the bloody front door of the bloody building, shouldn't it? Not way back there at the gate.

But despite her protests, the hired cabbie had just grinned good-naturedly, said something about another lord being expected in the village as he unloaded her trunk, then tipped his hat and driven away. All while she'd been standing there as the thunder rolled closer, getting more and more irritated as her demands were ignored.

Jade wasn't used to being ignored, and it rankled.

But, she also wasn't used to pouting, so she'd heaved a sigh —and then heaved her bag atop her trunk—and bent to lift one end of said trunk. It wasn't that heavy, and she'd had years of exercise to strengthen her muscles.

Still, she continued her grumbling as she locked her elbows and began to drag the thing up the gravel drive, hoping some enterprising servant would see her and come running to help.

But as she approached The Cottage, she realized the adorable name wasn't as modest as she'd hoped. Her Aunt Mary had married a Scottish lord, and Uncle Argus wasn't poor. Jade had, frankly, expected The Cottage to be a Lowland estate with a quaint name, conjuring images of bucolic oinking and rosy-cheeked milkmaids and—and—chickens and whatnot.

Jade could admit she knew little of country life.

But, upon delivery by that possibly deaf driver, Jade realized the name of her destination *wasn't* modest; the damned place really *was* a cottage.

Sighing, she dropped the trunk and straightened, stretching her back as she took in the view. The place was certainly quaint-with-a-capital-Q, with the thatching and the cheerful late-summer blooms in the window boxes and the white-washed walls and huge chimney. Was the place modernized inside, or had Uncle Argus invited her on some sort of medieval outing?

The thought of sponge baths—when hot running water awaited her back in London—made Jade frown, but she knew she wouldn't be here long enough for it to really matter. That's why her trunk was so light; she'd packed only for a few days, knowing her trusted managers at the office could direct business well enough in her absence. Here, she intended to march inside, give Uncle Argus a firm piece of her mind—*ai-ya!* Marriage by proxy *was* medieval!—and be on tomorrow's train south to London again.

Of course, she'd been planning on having a servant's help with getting back to the train station. And getting the trunk into The Cottage, for that matter. She might've left the thing, except for those heavy, dark clouds...

Taking a deep breath, Jade locked her hands in the small of her back and did a deep backbend. The air here was...well, surprisingly perfect. The Cottage sat on a small rise overlooking the Solway Firth, and from here Jade could see a little path leading down the cliffs to what must be the beach. Today the surf was loud, thanks to those fast-moving rain clouds, and she was glad to have shelter so close by. But the salt air had always put her at ease, and the sound of the waves was as comforting as a hug.

Perhaps Uncle Argus had guessed that, when he'd instructed her to meet him here by the eighteenth. His letter—which she had ripped in half in anger, then shoved into her bag solely to wave under the man's nose—had said he planned to offer her explanation. But the only explanation Jade wanted to hear was how he was planning on *undoing* this mess.

Marriage by proxy? She'd never heard of anything so ridiculous!

The salty sea air no longer seemed quite so comforting, and the first heavy splat of raindrops matched her mood as, grumbling, she bent to lift her trunk once more.

Uncle Argus *knew* she didn't want to marry! It was the entire bloody point of her taking on a silent partner until she could access the remainder of the inheritance he was ostentatiously overseeing, and buy out the mystery man. It had galled to offer partnership for sale, certainly, but was better than the alternative her guardian had suggested:

Marriage.

Yes, marriage to another man *would* keep her family's money out of slimy Lord Buthert's hands, assuming the spoiled lordling intended to force her into marriage as he'd been hinting. But when Argus had originally suggested the idea, Jade had tried to—as calmly as possible—explain that would still land her with the problem of the inconvenient husband.

As she'd explained to The Scot the other night in his hotel room, she didn't want to be married to *anyone*, if it meant giving up control. Unfortunately, that thought reminded her of how deftly she'd allowed the man control over *her*, and how she'd damn near swallowed her tongue a few days later when she'd seen him at the club.

Cheeks heating, and still grumbling, she arrived at the porch of The Cottage, adorably protected by an adorable portico. And she just couldn't seem to make herself care about the gouge she'd just put into the adorable gravel driveway on the way here.

Huffing with irritation, and wishing she had an umbrella, she stomped up to the front door and knocked loudly.

A full bloody minute went by before she heard sound on the other side of the portal. *Ai-ya*, were the servants as quaint as the rest of this place?

But the man who eventually yanked open the door was no servant.

"It's about fooking time you got here, auld man—"

It might've been funny, the way his mouth snapped audibly shut when he saw who was standing—chilled, damp, bedraggled—under the portico. *Might* have been, were Jade not staring up at him with that same sense of doom.

Blond curls. Laughing blue eyes—wide first in surprise, now softening in pleasure. Wide, expressive lips curling into a smile of genuine delight as he looked her up and down. He wore a kilt today, in muted greens and blues, befitting the wild Scottish coast behind her, and his sleeves were rolled to display shockingly bare forearms.

The Scot.

Her opponent on the strip.

Her husband.

...Assuming this marriage was legal.

Of course, she'd been prepared, had she not? Oh, not for *seeing* him here in Scotland—she'd expected to be meeting Uncle Argus for an argument--but her uncle's letter had named him, and she'd recognized him as the man she'd crossed swords with.

And the man she'd crossed swords with was also the courtesan she'd hired.

Cameron MacKay, darling of Society, lazy slugabed charmer who mooched from both sides of his family...was really The Scot, famed giver-of-pleasure, who taught her about desire and urged her to take her own virginity.

When he'd removed his mask at the fencing club a few days ago, and she'd realized who she'd been dueling, Jade had almost vomited.

In horror, obviously.

She'd made a hasty retreat to a private dressing room, where she could change into the costume of a maid she wore to come and go through the club's back entrance, and asked the concierge for the name of her opponent.

Cameron MacKay... The Scot...

And now possibly her husband?

Oh, hell.

The man's easy smile had turned downright sensual, and he rested his bare forearm against the edge of the door he held open, strong fingers wrapped around the wood. The last time she'd seen his hand bare of those garish red leather gloves, it had been pumping lewdly at his own cock in the mirror, moments before he'd come in thick white strands of—

Stop thinking about it.

Too late. She pressed her thighs together and tried to frown up at him, ignoring the way she suddenly wanted to run her palm along his bare skin.

"Well, Treasure," he all but purred, "I have to admit *ye* werenae who I was expecting to see."

Treasure. The reminder he still didn't know who she was had her frown deepening. "Will you invite me in, sir? You might not have noticed, but it is emphatically raining."

He made a show of peering out around the portico. "This? Nay, 'tis merely a bracing sea mist." On cue, thunder rolled, but he didn't blink before continuing, "A *loud* bracing sea mist."

She huffed. "Let me in, MacKay."

He grinned and stepped out of the door, allowing her to bustle past him as he bent to easily hoist her trunk and bag. He stomped inside and kicked the door closed as she stood in the foyer and removed her gloves as she looked around.

The Cottage wasn't medieval, but it *was* old-fashioned. From here she could see the dining room and the single parlor. There was a long hall toward the back of the house, leading to what she had to assume was bed chambers, seeing as how there was no upper level.

The noise her trunk made when it hit the ground startled her, and she swung about to see him grinning at her. His good humor in the face of this nonsense just made her more irritated.

"Dare I be flattered ye've learned my identity and tracked me down?" he asked, and he didn't bother disguising the hopeful note in his voice.

She hated that her body reacted to it. *Focus!* The way her stomach went all squiggly and her core pulsed was entirely inconvenient. She couldn't *afford* to be aroused by this man!

Why not? You were definitely aroused by him once, and no harm was done.

Ai-ya, that was before she was supposedly *married* to him!

"Don't be flattered, MacKay," she barked, irritated at herself *and* him. "I'm here to see your father."

Still eying her, he murmured, "Lucky bastard. Well..." He sighed, affected a dejected stance, and brushed past her on his way to the parlor. "Come in. I just poured myself some tea, and was debating between whisky—for the chill—or more sugar, because ye can never go wrong with more sugar. Can I pour ye either?"

The parlor was…adorable. The Cottage really *was* living up to its name, with the bucolic adorableness visible in each line. There were heavy rafters, a small fire in the hearth, and two sofas and a pair of chairs arranged cozily, surrounded by bookshelves and cabinets.

Between the two chairs, a small tea set stood, along with a pile of what looked like shortbread on a plate.

She cleared her throat. "Just tea, please." Although the extra sugar *did* sound delightful.

He was crouched in front of a low cabinet, and when he rose, he carried an extra tea cup and saucer. "Ah, I thought she stored them here," he said as he waggled the place setting at her and moved toward the teapot.

"She?" Jade asked weakly, pleased to already be drying from the warmth of the fire.

"The housekeeper. She lives in the village, but ensures The Cottage is up to standards before I arrive. She even left oyster stew on the stove, and I'll admit, it and the fresh bread smell divine."

Jade cautiously sniffed the air, and yes, there *was* something delicious somewhere nearby. He turned, the cup and saucer cradled in his overlarge hands, and caught her smelling his house.

Guiltily, she reached for the tea and took a too-large gulp to calm her nerves.

It didn't work.

"Please, sit, warm up." He gestured her toward one of the chairs. "Shortbread?" he asked as he flopped, effortlessly graceful, into the other and reached for his own cup. "Something stronger?"

The way he waggled his brows led Jade to guess he was suggesting something naughty, but she kept her back straight as she sat. "No, thank you." The tea actually was quite good. "The housekeeper isn't here now?"

"Nay," he said cheerfully. "We're all alone. I even managed to boil the water myself." He lifted his cup in salute.

A mocking reply died on her tongue as she realized what he'd said. "Alone?" she repeated hoarsely, shakily lowering the saucer. "Where's Uncle Argus?"

"Ah."

That was all he said: ah. He said "ah," sort of disappointedly, and crossed one long leg over the other as he twisted to place his cup on the table beside him.

Ah.

Jade absolutely refused to allow her gaze to drop below his knees, where his bare calves beckoned.

Her gaze insisted on disobeying.

Finally, he took a deep breath, which stretched the cotton of his shirt under his waistcoat. "I'm having a terrible, truly disappointing thought. Might I assume ye are Jade? My...bride?"

"Truly disappointing?" she repeated wryly, careful to place her own cup on the table before her hands betrayed her nervousness. She twisted them together in her lap. "That is disheartening."

"Disappointing, Treasure, because it means ye're strictly off-limits." He winked.

Oh, damn.

That wink...did he *want* her to be on-limits?

Ai-ya! Don't flatter yourself! He's a flirt, a charmer!

That he was.

She cleared her throat. "I am Miss Jade Thacker. My Aunt Mary is married to your father. That makes us cousins."

He was lounging in the leather chair, one leg thrown languidly across the other, his hands steepled in front of him as he studied her. It was an utterly inappropriate introduction, especially to one's relative. Or husband.

But it's not like this is the first time you've met the man, right?

Right.

Finally, he smiled. A sudden, blazing smile with no little amount of wickedness. "Oh, we most certainly are no' cousins, Miss Thacker," he murmured, the way his gaze raked her leaving no mystery to his thoughts. "I've been having all sorts of no'-at-all-cousinly thoughts about ye, Treasure."

Oh.

Oh, *my*.

Judging from the way his chin dipped, he knew exactly the effect his words had on her.

The thought he might've said such a thing just to fluster her, just to get the upper hand, made Jade's irritation spike again. The man was known throughout London—and especially in Uncle Argus's letters—to be a wastrel, good only for seducing women!

That's all he was doing now; flirting with her to get what he wanted.

What did he want?

And let's be honest here; you're ready to give it to him, yes?

No!

No, definitely no.

Maybe we should hear what it is before we "definitely no" anything.

Still no. She wasn't going to be manipulated by a set of gorgeous dimples and a muscled set of forearms and thick legs which reminded her of—

Focus!

"I'm not your Treasure," she snapped, reflexively. "Don't call me that."

"No," he murmured, his gaze hooded as he studied her. "According to my father, ye're my wife." Without giving her time to react to that, he pushed himself to his feet, startling her. "Would ye like a tour?"

CAM WAS OFF-BALANCE, and he'd long ago learned the best thing to do in such circumstances was to off-balance as many of those around him as possible.

Hence his outrageous flirting.

Which was, admittedly, not too difficult to manage.

God Almighty, but his Treasure was beautiful! With her unusual eyes spitting gray sparks, and two spots of color high on her cheeks, she looked the same way she'd looked that night in his hotel room, draped across that chair...

If ye continue down Memory Lane, laddie, ye'll have to go find a heavy sporran to prevent tenting yer kilt.

Slowly, she stood, maintaining a dignified air of cold grandeur. He wasn't fooled.

"No, Mr. MacKay, I would *not* like a tour. Because I am not staying. It isn't at all proper, to stay here with you, and no one else."

Just to see how she'd respond to his teasing, he pointed out, "It's perfectly proper, since we're married."

"We are *not* married," she hissed. "You cannot possibly believe we are?"

Ah, anger. Well, too bad, because she was just a delight to tease, and Cam knew he'd continue trying to make her lose control.

Instead of answering her question, he shrugged, as if the situation didn't bother him.

She sniffed. "I will return to the village, and await your father at the hotel."

"What hotel?" He grinned. "I believe there's a set of rooms

over the pub, but they're often in use by one of the local whores."

He'd used the crudest term, trying to shock her, but to his surprise, her gaze went all...curious? She studied his features in what looked like speculation, and immediately he wondered what she thought of the activities which went on over the pub. Which had gone on in Cam's hotel room.

She'd liked it.

He swallowed, reminding his inconvenient cockstand of the need for a sporran.

"Besides," he croaked, then swallowed and tried again. "Besides, there's nae cart to carry yer luggage and ye."

"I'll walk." Her attitude had mellowed somewhat.

"In the rain?"

Almost in unison, the pair of them cocked their ears to the sound of the rain pounding against the seaward-facing windows. The thatch muffled the sounds from above, of course, but the drumming was still suddenly loud.

"Your bracing sea mist, was it?" she asked drily, then sighed. "Well, I've been wet before."

"That's what she said."

The quip escaped his lips before he could stop it, and to his surprise, her eyes widened in understanding and her lips twitched before she turned away. Turned away to escape him, or turned away to hide her response to his ribald humor?

God help him, he liked Miss Jade Thacker, and her futile attempts at remaining in control, more and more.

Impulsively, he reached for her hand. She stiffened, but didn't pull away.

"Stay, Jade," he entreated quietly. "At least for dinner. When the rain stops, I'll carry yer trunks myself."

He could see her waffling. "Mr. MacKay, I don't think—"

"Then dinnae think," he interrupted her. "And please, call me Cam."

She blinked. "What?"

"Cam. My name." He tugged her slightly closer. "Well, it's Cameron, of course, but nae one calls me that except for my mother's husband, and then only when he's sneering at me. Och, and my father, when he's trying to sound stuffy," he added, remembering the damn letter which got him here in the first place.

"It's not proper," she breathed, her head tipped back to study him.

"Of course it is." He tried a smile. "Seeing as how we're married."

Those two spots of color returned to her cheeks, but she seemed more confused than angry. "We're—we're not married."

He shrugged. "Cousins?"

She swallowed, and swayed closer. "We're not cousins," she whispered.

Lowered lids, flared nostrils. Her tongue darted across her lower lip, her fingers tightened around his.

He knew the signs of arousal. Knew she was as affected by this nearness as he was.

"Lovers, then," he murmured, remembering the way she tasted.

She jerked back. Jerked hard enough she might have stumbled in her haste to get away from—from him? Or from his words? Luckily, he had a hold on her hand, and reached out with his free one to steady her.

Before she had a chance to insist they weren't lovers— which they weren't—and never could be lovers, he hurried to distract her.

"I'm remembering, that night ye came to me, Treasure." He kept his voice nonchalant, even as his thumb unconsciously caressed her upper arm. "Ye said ye wanted to lose yer virginity on yer terms, because yer guardian was likely to marry ye off to a spoiled lord or a lazy layabout who wouldnae challenge ye. Can I assume ye meant me?"

"You are not a spoiled lordling."

It took a moment to process the insult, and then Cam began to chuckle. "So I *was* the lazy layabout ye meant?"

With a sigh, she pulled her hand from his, but didn't step away. "I meant you, *Cam*. Your father's letters have been...full of complaints."

Still chuckling, he squeezed her upper arm before dropping his hold. "I can imagine exactly what he's said. No ambition, no responsibility." It was a façade he'd been careful to maintain over the years, out of sheer stubbornness.

Her head was cocked to one side, studying him. She really *did* look like a prim and proper miss today, didn't she? That blouse so high up her neck she looked as if she might choke, the double row of buttons on her jacket hiding her tempting breasts. No one who saw Miss Jade Thacker would guess she was the beguiling midnight Treasure who'd invaded his dreams for the last week.

"Yes," she finally said. "Something like that. Why does it not bother you, to hear his opinion?"

Cam shrugged and stepped aside, turning so as to invite her to follow him toward the dining room. "Because I've heard it for years, from him and from my mother's family."

In fact, he'd done his best to cultivate it, because that was so much easier than arguing. It wasn't worth the headache, to show them how wrong they were.

"But it's not true," she mused quietly, stepping out of the parlor. "You have a successful business—"

His laughter stopped him in his tracks, so suddenly she bumped into him. He whirled about to steady her, still laughing, and she stepped back in surprise.

"What's wrong?" she demanded.

Still chuckling, he shook his head. "A successful business?

Ye mean being The Scot?" *Remember, she thinks ye a true courtesan. Knows nothing of yer vow.* "I dinnae pay taxes on that income, Treasure."

He winked lewdly, but to his surprise, she frowned.

"Why not?" she asked. "You are selling a valuable commodity, and clearly it is enough to keep you in high style—parties and fencing clubs and your father says you have a fine townhouse, although I cannot imagine why he'd think that would sway me, when I'm quite comfortable on my own."

How'd she know about his membership at the London Fencing Club? "A 'valuable commodity'? Is that what ye call it?"

"Certainly." She nodded briskly, and he could see how she would be a formidable businesswoman. "Women sell such commodities all the time."

"Aye," he drawled, "but whores dinnae pay taxes either."

"I meant brides."

Her quiet reply rattled him, reminding him of why she'd sought him out in the first place. She hadn't wanted to sell her virginity—either to her guardian's lazy bastard son or to a spoiled lordling—so she'd claimed it herself. Is that what she was thinking of when she spoke of "selling commodities"?

He was more flustered than he admitted, because he found himself saying, "I dinnae keep the money."

Her gaze sharpened and she cocked her head in that curious style of hers which made him feel...well, really *looked at.*

"You didn't keep the money I gave you?"

Bloody hell, he hadn't meant to admit that. Rallying, he swept a hand toward the simple dining room. "Have dinner with me, Jade. Surely the rain will stop soon."

Thank fook she didn't pursue her earlier questions, but instead glanced toward the seaward windows, through which absolutely nothing was visible, thanks to the aforementioned rain.

"I'm beginning to doubt that," she murmured.

He shrugged, surprisingly desperate to get her to stick around. "Then stay the night. There's only the one furnished bedroom, because I never entertain when I'm here."

Her thoughts were hidden as she studied him. "This is your home?"

"The Cottage is mine, aye, but I dinnae live here. I assumed Da chose it as a meeting place because it was easier than coming down to London." He hurried to assure her, "Ye can have the bedroom, I'll sleep on the sofa in the parlor."

Her gray eyes tracked across his face, as if looking for the truth. "And where *is* your father? The letter I received—the letter explaining I am married to you, now—told me to meet him here, today."

"Aye," he sighed, rubbing the back of his neck. "His letter to me said the same. But when I arrived last night…" He held out both hands, palms up. "Nae word. I strolled down to the village today to learn Mrs. Higgins—the housekeeper—had notice from Da that The Cottage would have two visitors starting today. Hence the oyster stew. Which still smells delicious."

He could tell from the way her lips twitched that she wasn't completely unaffected by his hint toward the dinner table.

"Two visitors?"

He hummed. "I assumed he meant himself and me."

"Yet, he's not here." She made a show of peering about. "He might be hiding."

Smiling, he jerked a thumb toward the back of The Cottage. "Well, I havenae checked the storerooms."

"Under the bed?" she asked solemnly.

"It's possible the rain delayed him." The storm *was* wicked.

Her chin dipped. "Or he's set us up."

Aye, it was a suspicion which had beset Cam as soon as he'd opened the door and seen her beautiful—if angry—face.

Da, ye sorry son of a bitch, what in the name of Creation are ye thinking?

The answer came back loud and clear:

Cam was supposedly married to this tempting creature before him, and now Da had arranged for the pair of them to be stuck—together, alone—in a house with only one bed, at least overnight.

No consummation?

His father was a crafty arsehole, certainly.

But *this* crafty?

Cam had no idea what Miss Jade Thacker was thinking... but when she smiled, his mind—which had been whirling with possibilities—ground to a halt.

God Almighty, but her smile was perfect. She was always so in control, so to see her smile like this—part mischievous, part shy—was downright charming. And he was a man who specialized in charming.

That smile reached down into his gut and *pulled*.

No consummation.

"Cam," she said in a throaty voice, "did you say there are oysters for dinner?"

CHAPTER 5

JADE NEVER COULD TOLERATE A MYSTERY.

It was why she hired investigators when the insurance company declared a loss "an act of God"; it was why the fact her new partner refused to use his name on documents galled her so bloody much; and it was why she hadn't walked away from The Cottage last night.

Because with one little sentence, Cam MacKay had become a mystery.

What did he *mean*, he hadn't kept the money she'd paid him? Lady Melton had told her the amount—either in cash, or in baubles—The Scot demanded for an evening of pleasure, and Jade had brought it with her.

She'd woken in his arms when dawn was just a hint in the eastern sky, surprised she'd fallen asleep in the stranger's arms. Because no matter what they'd shared the night before, The Scot *was* a stranger to her. Wasn't he?

Her dressing had been the quietest she'd ever managed—half-terrified, half-excited he'd wake and she'd be forced to have a conversation with him after holding his gaze in the mirror and orgasming on his demand—and her fingers had closed around that wallet of money.

She'd come to his room to lose her virginity, to experience pleasure. While it hadn't gone quite as she'd imagined, it was impossible to deny both of those things had happened, and he'd been brilliant at putting her at ease. It was simple to place the wallet beside the dildo and the dog-eared copy of *A Harlot's Guide*—the reminder of what she'd done with that still made her breath hitch and her thighs quiver—and slip out of the room.

I dinnae keep the money.

So why had he demanded it? What did he do with it?

A mystery.

And Jade was definitely intrigued.

Unfortunately, she didn't sleep well the night after her arrival at The Cottage. Oh, Cam's bed was quite comfortable, and the rain had become a constant background noise which was almost soothing.

But it was *Cam's bed*, that was the problem. It was his bed, it smelled of him…and he wasn't in it. Of course, it was almost midnight before she was able to determine *that* was the root of her issue. She wanted him in the bed with her.

Holding her.

Pleasuring her.

Somewhere in the adorably bucolic home, a clock had struck midnight when she'd huffed in irritation, kicked her way out of the cozy coverlet, and yanked up her nightgown.

Yes, it was likely considered rude to pleasure oneself while borrowing the bed of one's host, but when just the *memory* of said host could make her hot and needy, there was no hope for it.

So Jade had planted her heels on the mattress, spread her knees, and touched herself. She'd touched herself the way *he* had, tugging at her nipples, slicking her wetness through her curls, trying to convince herself it was his tongue, wishing she had that thick ivory dildo again... And eventually, she'd orgasmed.

It had taken too long, and hadn't been nearly as satisfying as when he'd met her gaze in the mirror and commanded she come for him. But at least she'd been able to sleep after.

And this morning, she was determined to solve the mystery which was Cam MacKay.

She found him in the kitchen, which wasn't mysterious in itself, but was odd.

"Good morning." He was beaming as if a night on the sofa had agreed with him. "Hungry?"

"Starved," she agreed good-naturedly. The two of them being here together was an unusual situation, to be sure, but she wasn't the shy and retiring type, was she? She *needed* to understand him. "What did Mrs. Higgins leave us to break our fast?"

Cheerfully emphatic, Cam waved last night's leftovers. "Bread. I'll toast it. Butter or jam?"

The rain still hammered at the windows, and Jade had to admit a breakfast of toast and jam and tea sounded lovely. "Both please. I'll start the tea."

They worked in companionable silence. Jade had to stop herself from blurting out questions, knowing he'd just deflect them. She *wanted* to know more about his business dealings, and how he could afford not to keep the money women paid him—*and why!*—but the more time she spent in his presence, the more she understood another truth:

She wanted to know more about Cam because, well...she *liked* him.

It was surprising, definitely.

She liked his smiles, she liked how preternaturally cheerful he always seemed to be. But that cheer hid something else, and she found herself smirking more than once at his sharp wit.

They "dined" in the kitchen, standing near the warm stove, sipping their tea.

As Cam bit into his fourth piece of toast, Jade turned her attention to the window. This faced the rear of the house, so the rain appeared to be coming at an angle instead of directly against the glass.

"Well, I think it is safe to assume neither of us is planning an excursion to the village?"

He blinked in what seemed surprise, and hurried to swallow. "*I'm* no'. It's warm and dry in here, at least until the thatch begins to give out. But if *ye're* still intent...?" He lifted his heavily sugared tea and raised a brow at her over the lip of the cup.

Shrugging, she sipped at her own tea to hide the way her lips seemed to want to curl in his presence. "I'm content to remain until the rain stops. What do you *mean*, 'until the thatch gives out'?" Her eyes darted upward. "Is the only thing protecting us from being drenched a few strands of hay?"

He finished off his tea and gifted her with a smile as he began to clean up. "Try several feet of thatch, Treasure. Have ye no' been under real thatch before?"

For a spoiled Society fop, he certainly didn't mind tidying his own mess, did he? For that matter, he'd washed their dishes last night as well, and stored the remainder of the meal in the icebox, as if he were used to doing for himself.

"I didn't think 'real thatch' still existed," she admitted dryly. "We're in the modern era, you know. Electricity and running water and all that."

"Aye, and the comforts are always—well, a comfort, when I return to London. But here on the Firth..." He shrugged and plucked her empty cup from her hand to dunk it in the basin, where he'd poured hot water in with the cold. "Sometimes it's nice to remember simple pleasures, aye? And the scenery *is* verra beautiful."

Her lips curled as she glanced toward the window once more. "I'll take your word on that. Now, about these *simple pleasures…*"

His head whipped around so quickly she couldn't hide her snicker. When he saw it, his expression eased from curious to contrite.

"Och, so ye've learned to tease me as I've been teasing ye, eh? Here's me thinking ye had some 'simple pleasures' of yer own in mind…"

His sigh sounded so forlorn, she had to stifle a giggle. She managed to clear her throat and plaster on a stern expression when she nodded solemnly. "I do. I had to engage in a bit of it myself last night."

The soapy teacup slid out of his hand and splashed into the basin of water. "What?" he croaked.

She hummed, pretending confusion.

When he turned, not bothering to wipe off his hands before he plunked them on his kilted hips, her eyes were drawn to his bare forearms.

"What simple pleasure did ye engage in last night, Miss Jade Thacker?"

Her gaze still riveted to his muscular hands, glistening with soap bubbles, she felt her tongue dart across her lips. She'd intended to tease him, but it had suddenly grown quite difficult.

"Treasure," he murmured, and took an aborted half step toward her.

Her gaze jerked back to his. "Food!" she blurted, pleased to remember the direction of her original teasing. "If we're going to be stuck here until the rain stops, and Mrs. Higgins cannot reach us, how will we eat?" She swallowed. "I spent some time thinking of recipes I could remember."

For a moment, his face fell, his lips forming a sort of disappointed "oh". But then he brightened and shrugged those remarkably wide shoulders as he turned back to the basin. "And what did ye remember, Treasure?"

"Well, I confess, my mother was not a cook, but I've spent my share of weeks aboard my father's ships, and the cooks were always willing to show me one hundred and one things to do with salt pork."

"That sounds like a terrible children's primer," he quipped to the dishes. "One Hundred and One Things to Do With Salted Pork, Dry Biscuits, and Rat Feces to Get That Finger Out Of Yer Nose, Young Man."

"You've been aboard a ship, I see," she said drily. "And have some experience with young lads? Do you have a son?"

The thought had started as a joke, but even as she said the words, a horrible hollow feeling settled into her stomach. *Might* Cam have a child? He was certainly rakish enough to have fathered a few dozen bastards, if the stories were to be trusted.

And why did the thought of him siring a bastard on another woman make her feel...bitter? No, not angry, but *angry*. This sickly feeling clawing through her stomach wasn't jealousy, it was certainty; Cam fathering a child on another woman was *wrong*.

Why? Because you think he should be fathering one on you?

Ai-ya, no! Absolutely not. She didn't want his children.

Right.

Right.

Only a moment had passed while she argued collectively with her subconscious, her libido, and her surprisingly vocal ovaries. In that time, he turned and offered her another one of those patented dimple smiles of his.

"Nay," he assured her easily. "Nae bastards for me."

"How can you be certain?" she snapped, even while berating herself inside. *What are you doing? Don't ask more questions! Not if you don't really want the answers!*

His grin slipped just slightly, and he shrugged again as he turned back to finish rinsing. "I ken." Then he cleared his throat. "My best friend has a son. A good lad, almost ten, a mirror image of my friend."

It seemed a safer subject. "Really?" She began to set the kitchens to rights as well as she could, as he told her of Malcolm Forbes, whose home was to the west, and the poor man's doomed courtship.

She found herself entranced, and by the time Cam finished the story about how Malcolm had been reunited with his Violet—after agreeing to tutor the son he never knew was his —Jade found herself breathing a relieved sigh. "That's lovely."

"Aye, I'm pleased for the lucky bastard." Cam was grinning as he dried his hands, and she had to admit, she liked how he didn't pretend formality on her behalf. "And I'll tell ye more stories, once the whisky comes out."

"Whisky?" She arched a brow. "Is that how we're spending our day?"

"Och, *nay.*" He winked. "I prefer brandy for day-drinking. But whisky loosens my tongue, ye ken, and without proper food in our bellies, ye'll likely die drunk, starving, and bored by my rambling stories."

Jade couldn't help it; she burst into laughter at his dramatic take on things. "We'll not starve, you poor man."

"Nay?" He wiped his brow in mock relief, brushing his curls back. "So ye ken more than just salt pork?"

Still chuckling, she brushed past him toward the door she correctly identified as a pantry.

"When I wasn't aboard a ship with my parents, we lived in a quaint little home—not as *quaint* as this place, but comfortable—near Liverpool. Our housekeeper kept the pantry stocked with certain supplies—ah!"

Beaming, she turned, a small sack of baker's sugar clutched in her hands. His arms were folded across his chest, his hip against the counter, one corner of his lips drawn up in a sort of lazy amusement as he studied her.

"Is it salt pork, Treasure?"

"Better." She smiled. "Last night I wracked my brain, and I am fairly certain I remember how to make simple sugar cookies—"

His whoop cut off her explanation, and when he lunged for her, she froze.

He caught her up, tightening his hold around her waist as he swung her in a circle and cried, "*Lead* with the cookie offer next time!"

For her part, Jade had frozen as he'd lifted her, crushing the fine sugar between them. The feel of his arms around her, the way she was pressed against him...her eyes fluttered shut on a silent inhalation as she tried to capture his scent.

After a long moment, she realized she was no longer being spun about, and slowly opened her eyes.

He was still holding her, just her toes touching the floor. The rest of her was supported by *him*. His arms were tight around her back, her hands pressed against his broad chest. She could feel his heart pounding as heavily as hers was.

And something hard pressed against the junction of her thighs.

His blue gaze was locked on her lips, and she could *feel* the heat, even if she hadn't seen it. He was looking at her the same way he had before he'd asked to kiss her, that night in the hotel room.

Her core ached at the memory of his fingers, his *tongue*, his words, and she silently begged him to ask the question again.

She knew what she'd say.

Yes.

Yes.

Please.

GOD ALMIGHTY, he was in trouble.

Cam knew he was holding his breath—the whole fooking world was holding its breath!—as he struggled to control his natural instincts.

He wanted her. He wanted her right here in the kitchen, up against the counter. He wanted her in the bedroom, he wanted her on the sofa, where he'd tossed and turned, imagining *this exact scenario*. He wanted her now, and he was beginning to suspect, forever.

But he couldn't have her.

Because once he did, they'd be well and truly married, and she didn't want that.

One kiss. She wants it as much as ye do.

That much was obvious. Jade was practically straining toward him, ready to meet his lips with hers. Could she feel how much he wanted her? And she wanted him despite it?

What could one kiss hurt?

Well, it could bloody well destroy his restraint, that was for certain.

She doesnae want to be married to ye. Try to remember that.

Swallowing, Cam forced himself to set her on her own feet, to release her. He tried for nonchalance in his tone, and knew he completely failed, when he cleared his throat and asked, "Cookies?"

She swayed, clearly not understanding, and he had to touch her upper arms. Just to steady her, of course.

"Jade? Ye ken how to make cookies?"

"You sound…" She shook her head and took a deep breath, then tried again. "You sound eager."

He likely did. Shrugging sheepishly, he forced himself to step back. "Dessert is my favorite food group."

She hugged the sack of sugar to her chest as she cleared her throat. "Dare I ask what a food group might be?"

"A group of food."

"Yes." She nodded. "I suppose I asked for that, really."

He grinned. "Cookies are my favorite types of food. My mother's cook used to let me help decorate them when I visited. I'll whip up the icing for ye."

Her own lips twitched, something between ruefulness and pleasure, as she held out the sugar. "You'll need this then. I'll start on the dough."

He didn't immediately begin to mix the sugar with the lemon juice and egg whites—it was too early in the process. Instead, he helped by preparing the area. While she gathered the ingredients, he found the board and pin used for rolling—deep in the pantry—and laid them and a bowl out for her.

Their earlier moment wasn't forgotten exactly, but as the moments passed in a helpful bustle, the silence turned... companionable. As she began to mix, she peeked over at where he greedily watched the dough form.

"You said you visited your mother home? Does that mean you didn't live with her?"

Cam took a moment to study the question from all angles before deciding that telling her of his past wouldn't be too dangerous. "When I was verra young, certainly. As ye likely ken, my da is a charming man. I like to think I get it from him."

She snorted softly, her lips curling, her attention on her work.

He smiled in return. "Ye might no' be impressed, but my mother was. The daughter of an earl, ye ken, who seduced a Scot who had nae interest in marriage. It was the scandal of the decade."

"She seduced him?" Jade cocked a brow at him, her hands methodically working the dough.

"They both agree on that. Da made it clear he wasnae marrying her, and my mother didnae care." He shrugged and grinned. "Now, let us move on, because nae one wants to focus on their parents' sex life, eh?"

She grinned. "Deal."

"My mother weathered the scandal, but my grandfather wasnae impressed by me, and when he found my mother a husband—a snooty baron who likes me as much as I like him—they all agreed it would be best for me to go off to school."

Her hands had stilled as she watched him. With lips turned down at the corners, she murmured, "Even your mother?"

Suddenly, Cam decided he'd better find a bowl for his icing. The hunt was easier than seeing the pity in Jade's intriguing eyes. "My mother was busy with her new family, and likely grateful I wasnae there to remind everyone of her folly."

"And so, when you visited, you spent time in the kitchens," she said softly.

"Och, it wasnae so bad!" He turned with a forced grin, the bowl in his hands. "I got to lick all the spoons, and learned self-sufficiency. Also, as I grew, the lasses were perfectly willing to help me perfect my *skills.*" He winked lewdly, leaving no guess what he meant. "My education, and both of my families, taught me to be a gentleman. But I dinnae *have* to be, and that is a blessing all on its own."

She cocked her head, studying him in that way that tended to make him uncomfortable, as if she could really *see*, really understand, him.

"Yes, that is a benefit, I suppose," she finally agreed, before she dumped the dough out on the board and reached for the pin. "Especially for a businessman like yourself."

Since she was treading dangerously close to where he didn't want to go, he propped his elbows on the counter and turned the conversation. "And ye? Ye mentioned a ship and a *quaint* cottage in Liverpool—"

"House. This is a cottage. I had a proper house," she corrected without looking up.

"Which sounds perfectly *adorable*"—he used her word from yesterday—"but I'd rather hear about yer life on ship. This was one of yer father's ships?"

Her gaze jerked up. "You know my father?"

He managed a nonchalant shrug, as if he hadn't researched thoroughly. It had taken only a few moments, yesterday, after learning her name, to put it together with what she'd told him at the hotel, and realize which business it was she owned.

Although the coincidence was *astounding*.

It was too bad they'd met under those circumstances—

Nay, nay, her presence in his hotel room that night would never be "too bad" in his memory. But if they *hadn't* met that way, if they'd met at a political rally or whatever ridiculousness she'd suggested, she might've known the *real* him. Might've understood his secret.

Might've been willing to learn *why* he knew all about Thacker Shipping.

But for now, he needed a way to keep her talking.

"Everyone kens of Thacker Shipping, aye? Ye being raised onboard a boat, and at the hotel that night ye spoke of yer father's business…"

Slowly, her shoulders relaxed as she finished rolling out the dough. "Yes, Thacker Shipping. It's mine now, although signing everything *J. Thacker* makes my life easier, since Father's name was John. Before he met my mother, he sailed with most of his voyages, but after I was born he contented himself with shorter Channel crossings. Here, do you want to cut out the cookies?"

"Aye, of course," he agreed eagerly, already reaching for the dough, as she began to roll the next batch. "How did he meet yer mother? She was Chinese, aye?"

Her lips tugged into a thoughtful frown as she studied him. He grinned, not wanting to admit he knew plenty about Thacker Shipping.

"Yer name is *Jade*, Treasure, and yer coloring..." He shrugged. "A good guess."

"Yes, it was." Thankfully, her suspicion eased. "My mother was the daughter of a very wealthy merchant in the Guangdong region. My father met her at a banquet given in his honor, and they fell madly in love."

As Cam carefully cut out increasingly rude shapes—without her noticing—Jade told a romantic tale of forbidden courtship, daring feats, and finally a grandfather won over by love. When her mother, Meilin, joined her father on the high seas, her merchant grandfather deposited an obscene amount of wealth in a London bank for his grandchildren, when they came of age.

"They only had me, you see, and so in a month, when I reach twenty-five, I'll finally have access to that money."

Which she would pour back into her father's—*her*—company. "I remember. And if ye can manage to hold off marriage until then, ye'll have yer control."

If she was currently married to him, it could still be annulled...considering neither had consented in the first place.

She snorted softly, but he couldn't tell if she was thinking of her supposed marriage to Cam. "The laws are favoring a woman to keep her inheritance, but I'd rather be certain."

As they baked first one batch of the cookies, then more, he asked her questions about Thacker Shipping, and found himself amazed by how she managed so much. Not because she was a woman, no; such an empire would've taxed *anyone's* organizational abilities. But she was enthusiastic and level-headed as she explained, even when he didn't quite understand the technical aspects of trade.

In return, she asked him about his years at school, and he found himself telling her of the friends he'd made; Malcolm, Keith, James, and even Crowe. He told her how they'd all been sent to Swinson's, and the other lads there had objected to mingling with bastards.

"You're all bastards?" she clarified with curiosity.

"Aye, and my mother was the only lady among our mothers. Our fathers—all lairds—sent us for various reasons, but finding each other was the best thing which could've happened to us." He knew his crooked grin wasn't quite convincing. "It's easier to fight bullies with friends at yer back."

"Malcolm was the friend you told me about?" She waited for his nod, then asked, "And the others? Do you still see them?"

"Keith made his fame as the Battling Bastard, Britain's bareknuckle champion. He was married a few months back." Cam leaned in conspiratorially. "To the Duke of Cashingham's little sister."

Jade, properly impressed, chuckled. "There's a story there," she quipped as she tested the first batch of cookies. "How about the others? These are ready to be iced, by the by."

Reaching for them, Cam gave his icing one last whip. "James Lindsey died ten years ago, murdered."

"Oh, Cam," she gasped, her fingertips resting on her lips. "I'm so sorry. That must have been so difficult for the rest of you. Were you all together for the funeral?"

Swallowing, Cam focused on flooding the cookies the way his mother's cook had taught him years before. This one—a set of perfectly round tits—only required painting a pair of nipples, but the next—a flaccid cock—would be more complex.

"Aye," he murmured, intent on filling in the scrotum with icing. "Except for Crowe."

"Where was he?"

Without thinking, he answered, "In prison for murder."

When she gasped again, he winced, realizing what he'd admitted, and glanced up with a rueful smile to see her horrified expression.

"Och, it was a decade ago, lass. I miss James"—*and Crowe*, although he would never admit that to Keith and Malcolm —"but he's at peace, and so am I."

"Is Crowe still in prison?" she whispered.

He forced a crooked smile. "No' anymore, which is why I'm glad to be hiding here in Dumfries, aye?" She didn't respond to the humor. "Och, lass, dinnae fret. Here, tell me, does this look like a vulva to ye?"

When he turned the plate to display one of his creations—complete with outlined folds and a delicate iced clitoris—she gasped for the third time. Only this turned into more of a choke, and it wasn't until he stood to pour her some water that he realized she was laughing.

"Cameron MacKay, did you style *all* of my cookies in—in *naughty* shapes?"

Och, she's using yer full name? Ye're in trouble, laddie!

He grinned unrepentantly. "Aye!" he admitted cheerfully. "Far more fun to put in yer mouth, eh?"

Still giggling, she darted forward and snatched up one of the cookies. "Then here, it's only fair *you* taste them first!"

And with that, she popped it into his mouth.

A flood of sweetness spread across his tongue, but he wasn't so distracted that he couldn't grab her wrist, holding her—and the cookie—in place. He bit through the confection, leaving the rest in her hand, making sure his lips brushed against her fingers.

This close, he could see her eyes change from gray to a

dark blue, and a soft shudder pass through her. As he chewed, he held her gaze.

"It's good, lass," he finally whispered, offering her a smile. "Verra, verra good."

Suddenly, an impish grin split her lips. "I'm so glad to hear you say that." And she dropped her eyes to the remains of the cookie she held.

Instinctively, his gaze dropped as well, and he saw her fingers wrapped around a pair of bollocks.

She was holding one side of the cookie he'd cut out to look like an erect cock.

The shaft was missing, and the taste in his mouth suddenly turned sour. "Did ye just feed me a penis cookie?"

Her grin grew, and she dropped one eyelid in a devilishly teasing wink. "You took a big bite of the poor thing. How did it taste?"

"I'm no' answering that now."

Solemnly, she nodded. "And risk ruining your reputation. I understand."

God help him, when she giggled, he couldn't control his humor any longer, and began to chuckle as well. There they stood, her holding a half-eaten cock cookie, and him holding *her*, laughing together.

And Cam knew he shouldn't be having this much fun.

Forget being in trouble, laddie. Ye. Are. Fooked.

CHAPTER 6

BY THE THIRD day of rain, Cam believed he'd gone past *fooked* and into *damned* territory. But not like regular damned... This was the *damnéd* of poets, when they have to add in an extra syllable just to tell you how *damnéd* you really are.

And it all began and ended with Miss Jade Thacker.

His maybe wife.

Nay, she's no' yer wife yet, because ye havenae fooked her yet. She's still yer bride.

Not a helpful distinction.

Because by the third day of being trapped inside with her, Cam was well on his way to being in love.

But whatever his feelings for her, he was a gentleman. He *knew* what she wanted, and it wasn't him; it wasn't *any* sort of husband. And the moment Cam made her *his*, the way he ached to do, she'd lose any sort of leverage to have this marriage annulled.

So keep yer hands to yerself.

It was difficult. Jade was unknowingly making it *more* diffi-cult, with her smiles and teasing winks and the way her arse moved whenever she walked away and how sometimes she'd bend over to pick up something and Cam's cock would jump to attention without a thought.

Hell, the woman could likely pick her teeth or dig in her ear and Cam would find it erotic.

Erotic teeth picking. I dinnae recall that entry in A Harlot's Guide.

He'd found an edition of the book in the study the night before last. Well, confession: he'd gone looking for the thing, recalling he'd left it at The Cottage years ago. It was a helpful little tome, and he'd long ago made it a point to keep a copy wherever he stayed.

Well, last night he'd needed something to take his mind off the fact Jade was sleeping in his bed, and figured a good hand-frigging was necessary.

But it hadn't worked, because all the illustrations reminded him of Jade, and the thought of *her* in those positions had been enough to make him come. Twice.

And he *still* tossed and turned on the hard sofa.

Unfortunately, Jade didn't seem nearly as affected as he was. Despite being indoors for so long, she still seemed cheerful, issuing commands to him he was happy to go along with. He was an easygoing sort of fellow, and she was used to being in control of her company. And frankly, he'd eat hot coals just to have her smile at him, so…

Aye, he was *damnéd*.

That first day, after finishing the cookies, they went hunting for more food, assuming that would be the priority. Luckily, Mrs. Higgins had ensured the icebox was well-stocked, and the pantry had more basics. They had sandwiches for luncheon, and for dinner they heated the remainder of the stew from the night before.

Although Cam didn't need any *oysters* to help him in the cockstand department, *thankyeverramuch*. Thank fook Jade apparently didn't know the rumors of shellfish being an aphrodisiac, because he didn't think he'd be able to stand her teasing looks as they ate.

The following morning, she pulled out a book of recipes, and the two of them had made bread together. It was a messy process, and the result wasn't nearly as light and airy as the loaf Mrs. Higgins had left them, but they would survive.

Since the oven was hot, Cam talked her into making another batch of cookies.

"What? You've finished the batch we made yesterday?"

He'd pretended to be offended. "*Ye* helped eat them, lass."

"Only the cock-shaped ones, since you refused to touch them."

God Almighty, but the sound of the word *cock* on her lips went straight to his groin. He must've made a little sound of protest, because her smile grew.

"And besides," she drawled. "I ate mine daintily. You were the one who made a show of licking all the icing off the one shaped like—what was it?"

Cam closed his eyes on a groan. "An arse, Treasure," he admitted in a strained voice.

"Oh, yes, a pair of perfectly plump cheeks, I remember. You licked them clean, which was most uncouth."

Uncouth? Cam knew the sight of her delicately nibbling at the tip of an erect cock would keep him awake again that night.

"What if I promise to stick to more conventional shapes?" he asked desperately. "Squares, circles, rhombuses?"

"Rhombuses?" She smirked. "Rhombi?"

Dammit, he wanted more cookies! "Rhombedes."

She was outright giggling now. "*What?*"

"Octopus has a Greek stem, so the correct plural is *octopodes*. I'm not sure about rhombus."

She laughed, and pulled out the sugar. "Absolutely no rhombuseseses. Now that I know your preferred cookie shape, I'm going to try my hand at cutting them into naughty shapes. *You* get to stir and roll today, *I'm* cutting."

What followed was an hour of laughter and jokes as he gave her impromptu anatomy lessons and she made a point of cutting everything correctly. He might've been able to control himself, had she not demanded a reference guide, and then jogged to the sitting room to pull out that apparently not-very-well-hidden copy of *A Harlot's Guide.*

Cam's knees had gone weak, watching her consult the illustrations as she bent over the cutting board.

He doubted he'd forget the sight of her tongue poking out from between her lips, a smudge of flour on her cheek, as she concentrated on getting the outer labia of a cookie just so.

Cookies should *not* be erotic.

He'd made the shapes as a joke, but now... God help him, she'd turned the joke on him.

Luckily, she made plenty of shapes he was willing to eat, and they enjoyed the cookies throughout the day, as they made a simple dinner from ingredients in the icebox, and then organized the pantry and china closet.

It wasn't something he would've suggested, but she didn't leave him room for argument.

"Stop fussing, Cam! You can't just sit around on your hands for the rest of the day; you'll go mad! And the china needs dusting. Help me stack these saucers on the dining table, please. I think I saw some rags in the bedroom."

He pretended to object, even as he began moving things about. "First of all, those are my *handkerchiefs*, and my valet will challenge anyone who says differently to a duel. Second of all, I can *happily* sit on my hands all day."

Not that he would be doing exactly that; he had last quarter's profits to review, but of course he didn't want to do it where she could see.

She was already moving toward the hall. "Handkerchiefs *are* rags, and ask your valet if he prefers foils or broadswords."

Cam's laughter followed her through the house.

But The Cottage was small, and most of the bedrooms were unfurnished—hence his aching back from sleeping on the sofa. There was only so much they could organize or straighten or clean.

Which was why today, the third day of rain, the pair of them were standing in front of a cabinet in the parlor.

"Are ye certain ye'd rather no' just read books?" Cam asked with a wince, eyeing the collection of boxes. "There's quite a few along the other wall."

"We tried that already." Jade threw him a lewd wink. "Our literary tastes intersect in only one, very important book."

He swallowed, remembering how happily she'd exclaimed as she'd flipped through the pages of *A Harlot's Guide*. He shouldn't have been surprised she was familiar with the publication, but *God Almighty*, a man could only put up with so much in the erotic fantasy department.

"Nay," he managed weakly. "Perhaps reading isnae the best idea after all."

She nodded firmly and reached for the boxed set. "Chess?"

It was one of the only recognizable games some long-ago, well-meaning soul had left, but Cam wrinkled his nose. "Malcolm always despaired of my ability to sit still long enough to finish a game."

With a little chuckle, Jade twisted to place the game on a low table. "So what you're saying is I have a better-than-even chance of kicking your arse at chess. Got it. A definite maybe."

Groaning, Cam reached into the cabinet once more. "How about this one? It appears to be made up of small letters on squares. Ye place the letters out to make words."

"Make words?" she repeated doubtfully, peering over his

shoulder to see better, her breath fluttering in his ear. "That sounds...boring."

"Oh, I dinnae ken." He struggled to keep his tone nonchalant. "I can think of some interesting words."

Humming, she took it out of his hands. "Like 'titillate' and 'engorged'?"

God Almighty, did she realize what it did to him, hearing those words on her lips? "I was thinking more like..." His voice sounded strained, even to his ears. "'Rhubarb' and 'frigid' and 'sanctimonious'."

She was reading the instructional booklet. "No good," she muttered. "We only get seven letters. So *virgin* would work, but *virginal* or *insatiable* wouldn't. Ooh, look, if I spell 'brazen' along this side of the board, it's a triple-word score! That would make it...um...sixty-three points!"

There were points involved in this game? Cam was trying to follow her logic, but his mind kept getting stuck on the way her lips had looked when she'd said *insatiable*.

"The letters Q, X, J, and Z seem to be worth the most. I can't think of a word with all of those letters, but *quim* would be worth fifteen—"

"That's enough, lass," he blurted, as he snatched the box from her hands. "Let's see what else is available."

She shrugged, and her eyes sparkled with enough mischief to make him wonder if she knew how much trouble her innocent words were causing him.

"Here's another game I've never heard of."

She pulled out a large folded piece of canvas, painted with what looked to be big colored circles. "What is it?" he asked.

"It seems to be..." She trailed off as she pulled out a piece of cardboard with an arrow attached. "Oh, yes. Look, you spin this arrow, and then everyone puts their right foot on green."

"On the green dot?" He frowned. "That doesnae seem so difficult."

"But then you have to put your...left hand on blue. And your—let's see—right hand on green."

"But our right feet are already on green." This sounded dumb.

"Yes." She winked at him. "Imagine how twisted up we'd become."

And just like that, the image came to him; the pair of them attempting to balance as they followed the game's silly instructions, would be reminiscent of what he'd *rather* be doing. The pair of them, nude and glistening and panting, wrapped around each other in bed.

Abruptly, Cam stood, dragging her along with him. The stupid game fell from her fingers, and he couldn't stop himself from grabbing her hand, suddenly feeling as if the walls were too tight around him.

"Let's go for a walk," he blurted hoarsely.

Amused, she glanced at the window. "Have you forgotten it's raining?"

Desperate now, he took two steps toward the door before even looking toward the panes. "It's slowed down, aye?" The thunder had stopped that first day, and now... "Look, it's merely a drizzle." He tugged again. "Come along, lass, neither of us will melt."

"I'm not so sure of that," he thought he heard her mutter under her breath. But then she nodded. "It *is* getting a little tight in here. And getting wet won't hurt us."

Tight. Wet. God Almighty, he did *not* need to hear her use that sort of language.

"This way, then," he announced in loud relief, reaching for one of the three umbrellas in the stand beside the front door.

Chuckling, she joined him, and as he pulled open the door, shrieked a little in laughter as she tried to open her umbrella without getting wet. He handed her his while he struggled with hers, and she—still laughing—stepped out from under the portico.

He'd been correct; the rain *had* lessened today. Whereas yesterday it had beat steadily and relentless against the thatch and soaked ground, today the storm seemed to admit that perhaps it had been hasty in its "never-ending flood" threats, and it was considering petering off and having a lie down among the hills inland a bit, manifesting as a light drizzle here and there.

The wind was still steady, but it always was around this part of the coast. It whipped the remaining splatter of rain-drops in all directions; sometimes downward, often sideways, and on one memorable occasion, Cam swore he saw it raining *upward*.

But he was out of doors, and he was with Jade, and as he breathed deeply of the salty sea air, he felt himself calming, and knew this was what he'd needed.

She was the one to slip her hand through his, and he took it gratefully. With their palms pressed together, and rain soaking their wrists where the umbrella's protection didn't extend, he imagined he could feel her heartbeat.

Imagined it matched his.

Without discussing their destination, they both turned toward the cliffs, which overlooked the beach. It was only a short distance down, but Cam could see how muddy the path was, and didn't bother leading her toward it. Instead, they stopped with The Cottage to their backs, and their umbrellas in their hands, and peered out across Solway Firth.

When he was younger, right after Da had signed the prop-erty over to him, he used to peer out at the water with a tele-scope, watching the boats and imagining he could see clear to the other side, to the lassies sunning on the beach at Siloth.

Now, however, the Firth was a nasty churning of storm-swept gray with hints of blue on the tips of each wave.

Very much like Jade's eyes.

She said something, but the wind snatched it away from her. He turned to face her, the tips of their umbrellas bouncing against each other, since he refused to release her hand.

"What?" he yelled.

"It's lovely!" she bellowed in return.

His lips curled into a lazy smile, and he didn't bother turning to glance at the Firth again, but held her gaze. "It certainly is."

He wasn't sure if she heard him, or just was able to read the words. Either way, he saw her cheeks darken in a blush, and a small smile tugged at her lips as she lowered her eyes.

He wanted her. He wanted to taste her again, the way he'd done that night in the hotel. He wanted to claim her, to make her *his*... But at that moment, he'd settle for a kiss.

A kiss on a rain-soaked cliff overlooking a stormy sea. A kiss to tell her—to show her!—how special she was.

To him.

But...once he kissed her, could he let her go? Eventually, this storm would have to stop, and either Da would arrive to explain this mess, or Cam would be able to walk to the village and send a telegram north demanding *what in the everloving fook* his father had been thinking.

Eventually. Because all good things must come to an end.

And when this—this—this interlude, this being stuck in The Cottage with Jade Thacker, when this came to an end... If he'd kissed her, would Cam be able to let her go?

The way she wanted?

At that moment, a gust of wind tore the umbrella from Jade's grip. She twisted, but was only in time to see it tumbling away, smashing against the side of The Cottage before continuing its journey toward freedom.

Cursing, Cam stepped forward, trying to save her, but Jade surprised him.

Instead of hurrying under the meager protection his umbrella offered, she laughed. She laughed, and spun in a circle, the rain already plastering her blouse against her skin, outlining her corset beneath.

Under the thick kilt Cam wore, his cock decided perhaps it wasn't so chilly out here after all.

Because he'd thought Jade lovely before, but now... Now, seeing her with this much joy, this much unfettered passion... he was lost.

She caught him staring at her, and must not have seen his thoughts in his expression. If she had, she wouldn't have stopped laughing, wouldn't have stepped *closer*, close enough to gain protection from his umbrella, close enough to feel his warmth. Close enough he could see his hopelessly enamored gaze reflected in the raindrops clinging to her lips.

He wanted her.

He couldn't have her, because she didn't want him.

Remember the way she tastes.

God Almighty, did he.

Her tongue darted across her lips, catching those raindrops, and he was fairly certain he groaned aloud. "Jade," he began in a strangled voice, but then was at a loss of how to finish his thought.

She met his eyes, and smiled.

THREE DAYS. Three days, trapped in The Cottage with Cam, three days of him ignoring her hints and subtlety. Three days of working beside him, laughing beside him, teasing him, finding excuses to touch him.

And three nights of lying in his bed, *aching* with need,

unable to capture that breathless joy he'd so easily gifted her in that hotel room.

She wanted him, and she could tell he wanted her.

And she was tired of him being such a gentleman.

He was a rake, dammit, and it was time he start acting like one.

Standing there in the rain, gazing up at him, each raindrop touched her wet skin with a sharp prick of electricity. Each breeze felt like a gale, pushing her toward him. And she knew it was time to take matters into her own hands.

So when he murmured her name in that hopeless tone, she smiled. And stepped forward. And kissed him.

It was an awkward kiss for a few reasons.

One: it was colder out here than she'd expected, what with the soaked clothing.

Two: she wasn't—to be fair—particularly experienced in the kissing department, and this was the first she'd tried to initiate.

And Three: the recipient of her kiss had apparently entered the All-British Statue Mimicry Competition, and was making great strides—or rather, none at all—toward winning.

Damn.

Well, at this moment, she couldn't do a thing about numbers one and two, but *three...*

She was the proud owner of a leather-bound, fully illustrated edition of *A Harlot's Guide to the Forbidden and Delightful Arts*, and she'd read it cover to cover twice, before bookmarking her favorite pages and positions. Which she'd spent the last few years referring to in the dead of night, when the *need* became too great and she required release.

One thing the *Guide* was clear on was the appeal of a wet woman. Especially one who was bold enough to initiate a kiss.

She *would* be appealing, dammit.

Jade lifted her arms and wrapped them around his neck,

pulling herself closer, *plastering* herself against him... She knew she was soaking wet, knew she was dripping all over him, but hoped her gamble would pay off.

For a long moment, Cam continued his statue impression. Then, thank goodness, she felt him relax, loosen, surrender. As one of his large hands curled around her hip, she felt his lips part beneath hers, felt him rumble a growl which reached into the depths of her core and *pulled.*

In this position, she couldn't squeeze her thighs together to assuage the ache, so she did the next best thing—which she quickly realized was the *best* thing—in the circumstances; she pushed her pelvis against his, and felt the thick hardness she was hoping to feel.

As his lips claimed her in all the best ways, she remembered the way he'd looked, one of those hands wrapped around his thick cock, pumping as he'd commanded her to come. *Ai-ya*, that memory left her breathless. Or maybe it was the kiss.

With a whimper, she gyrated against him, trying to press that hardness against the top of her cleft, where she *needed* the pressure, needed his touch.

Another burst of wind startled her, and then raindrops were hitting her once more. She glanced down to see Cam had dropped his umbrella—because of the wind, or because he wanted both his hands free?—and shifted to stand atop it so it wouldn't join hers in blowing to oblivion. His free hand now cupped the back of her neck, pulling her closer to him, as his hold on her hip moved to her rear end, his strong fingers claiming her in the most delightful way.

But even as his kisses moved down her jaw to her neck, and Jade tipped her head back to the rain, reveling in the feel of his skin against hers, she knew it wouldn't be enough.

No, it wouldn't be enough, not until she could touch him, and he could touch *all* of her.

Cameron MacKay had ruined her.

She would never be satisfied without him.

"Treasure," he growled against her skin, the vibrations sending shudders through her. "Ye're so…"

Perhaps he finished his thought, and she couldn't hear him above the sound of the rain and her own pulse in her ears. Or perhaps he was as breathless and incoherent as she was.

She moaned in encouragement as his hand dropped from her neck to her chest, cupping one small breast through the wet cotton and corset. She wanted that, wanted more, but not here, surrounded by the fury of sea and sky.

He must've thought the same, because he broke away with a sound of protest. "Treasure," he groaned, pressing his forehead to hers. "We're soaking wet."

Instinctively pressing her thighs together, Jade agreed without thinking. "I certainly am."

And when he groaned again, he flexed forward in a movement she thought might've been instinctual. She grinned, knowing the power she had over this man, but inside, another part of her was slathering in anticipation of his directions.

"Come," she whispered, knowing he could hear her under the sound of the wind. "Come inside. With me."

When she took his hand, he stooped to pick up the umbrella, but followed wordlessly after her. And she knew she'd get what she needed.

CHAPTER 7

IN THE FOYER, Cam untangled his fingers from hers and took the time to refold the umbrella and place it in the stand to drip-dry. Then he turned his attention to Jade.

She was already shivering, her dark hair plastered to her pale skin, raindrops glistening on her cheeks. The sight made him want to kiss her again.

Dinnae be daft; literally everything makes ye want to kiss her again. Birdsong? Kissing Jade. Last quarter's profits? Kissing Jade. A broken arm? Kissing Jade. The maharajah's elephants? That's right, kissing Jade. Ye've got a one-track mind.

That had been Crowe's phrase for him, teasing Cam when they'd been in school. Or rather, not *tease*, because the man's wit was so dry it was practically parched, but still. He'd been right; Cam had a one-track mind.

One corner of his lips pulled up wryly. What could he say? He was a rake through and through, in spite of his vow.

But that wasn't going to warm her, because he wasn't going to let himself touch her again. But he *could* help her.

"Go get changed," he demanded, "before ye freeze to death." Her white blouse was plastered to her, and he wished he'd had the foresight to grab that jacket she'd worn her first day here. It would've offered protection from the rain...and from his gaze.

Her teeth were chattering when she grinned at him. "You as well. Do you have any idea how fine you look in wet cotton?" Her gaze raked across his shoulders. "I hadn't realized fencing was such sufficient exercise."

When had he told her he fenced? Cam shook his head, feeling water spraying from his hair. "I enjoy calisthenics and boxing as well. Now *go*."

He shooed her toward the bedroom, and when she peeked over her shoulder to give him a definite come-hither smile, he knew he was going to have to be stronger.

It wasn't an encouraging thought. He wasn't used to *refraining* from kissing women.

In the kitchen, he set a kettle of water to boil. Years ago, he'd had water pipes run to the kitchen to make Mrs. Higgins' life easier, but he was beginning to really regret not doing so to the small chamber off his bedroom which had been desig-nated the bathing room.

A hot bath sounded lovely right now, but what he likely needed was a *cold* one.

By the time the water was hot, he'd stripped from his wet shirt and kilt, and had tugged on a pair of trousers from his bag he'd moved out of the bedroom when Jade had moved in. It had been an uncomfortable experience, since apparently the cold dousing hadn't diminished his cockstand one bit. The idea of pulling a new shirt over wet skin made him shiver, so he hung a towel around his shoulders after he dried his hair as best he could.

Then, using one corner of the towel to protect his hand, he lifted the kettle and made his way toward the bedroom.

The door was shut, thank fook, so he couldn't see her changing. As much as he wanted to, he knew he *shouldn't*, not if he wanted to maintain control. Besides, the thought of those long legs, kicking out of the sodden skirt, or slipping into clean stockings, was going to keep him awake all night.

He took a deep breath and knocked. "Jade? I have some hot water for you to wash with. I'll leave it out here."

A moment, and then, "Could you bring it in, please?"

Wincing, Cam reached for the latch. But when he pushed open the door and stepped inside, his breath caught in his throat.

She hadn't changed into dry clothes.

Oh, she'd stripped from her wet things—Cam had glanced them hanging on the wall before his gaze had been dragged, almost inevitably, back to her—but instead of a dry gown, she'd donned a robe. A silk robe in pale purple, the kind meant to go on over a nightgown.

It wasn't designed for warmth. It was designed for showing off a woman's figure. And from the way she stood in the center of the room, her hands on her hips, her damp hair curling about her shoulders, she knew it.

God Almighty, he could see her nipples through the fabric, two tight little buds begging for his mouth.

"Are ye no' cold?" he blurted, then winced again, knowing perfectly well she *was* cold.

"Yes," she purred, beginning a slow stalk toward him, her hips swaying erotically. "But I can think of a way you could warm me."

Desperate to prevent her from doing something she would regret, Cam held the kettle out, between them. "Aye, I brought hot water, remember?"

She stopped in her advance, confusion flickering across her expression. "Put it on the table, then."

Like a schoolboy called to task by his bitter stepfather, Cam slid along the walls of the room to deposit his burden, then edged back toward the door, his eyes never leaving her, as if waiting for her to pounce. Maybe he *was*.

"Cam," she said in a low, confused voice. "You kissed me."

"Ye kissed me," he hurried to correct her. "I kissed ye back."

"Yes, but clearly you enjoyed it."

Oh *fook*. Her gaze had dropped to his trousers when she'd said this, and when her tongue dragged across her lips, he felt his pelvis jerk forward, as if tied to an invisible string.

"Lass, stop," he managed in a hoarse voice. "Ye dinnae want this."

Unreadable gray eyes flicked back to his. "Oh, but I do. I thought I'd made that very clear."

And that's when she untied her robe. Cam reached for the edge of the doorframe to hold himself steady, because when she lifted her hands to brush the silk from her shoulders, his knees went weak.

"Cam," she whispered, holding his gaze, "I *do* want this. I want you. I haven't been able to get that night out of my head, and the things you did to me. *For* me. I want to feel that way again."

Holy fook ye're fooking fooked so hard.

His fingers tightened around the doorjamb, the bite reminding him to be strong.

"Ye…" He swallowed, and tried again. "Ye dinnae want to be married, remember?"

"I want you," she repeated.

And that's when the robe fell off.

Cam's eyes closed on a curse, his dry throat working silently, but not before the vision across the room was burned into his mind.

Long, strong legs, taught stomach, pert tits standing proud, those nipples straining toward him…

He groaned and dropped his forehead against the wood of the door, knowing he couldn't resist her plea.

But he couldn't forsake his vow, either.

Eyes still closed, strong oak cool against his skin, Cam hoarsely commanded, "Get on the bed."

There was a rustle of fabric, and he could imagine the mattress bending slightly under her weight, imagine her long, firm limbs supporting herself…

"I'm ready," she murmured breathlessly.

He knew she was waiting for him, but couldn't weaken. Instead he squeezed his eyes tighter, trying not to picture her eager anticipation.

And failing.

He had to clear his throat before he spoke. "Lie back, Treasure." He waited a moment, then, "Are yer hands cold?"

A pause, then he heard, "Yes."

"Warm them," he ordered. "Put them in front of yer mouth, and blow on them." That's how he would warm them, if he could. "Curl them around each other, think of them in my hands."

He could hear her breathing, and he hummed in approval.

"Use them, now. Touch yer jaw. Drag yer fingers down yer neck. The places ye want my lips." He shuddered, eyes still clenched closed. "Can ye feel me, lass?" he asked hoarsely.

"I can," she whispered, sounding strained. "I want to feel your kisses. Here. Here. Here."

Dinnae open yer eyes, ye dobber. Dinnae open yer—

Too late.

How was he supposed to ignore the lure of *here here here*? He wanted—*needed*—to see where she was imagining his lips.

Holy fooking God, her fingers were splayed across the tops of her tits, dragging her touch back and forth as she stared defiantly at him.

Cam swallowed heavily and shifted his weight, his cock straining against the front of his trousers. His grip on the doorframe the only thing holding him upright.

"Yer nipples," he managed. When her eyes widened, he cleared his throat. "Touch yer nipples. Pinch them. Tug at—*Fook*, aye, like that."

She remembered the way he'd touched her in the mirror. Either that, or she was a fast learner who knew what she liked.

He watched her roll her nipples between both thumbs and forefingers, the little buds appearing painfully hard. Jade was chewing on her bottom lip, as if to hold in her moans.

"Nay, lass," he instructed. "I want to hear yer pleasure. Dinnae hide it from me."

With a gasp, her lip flew from between her teeth, and she arched upward, as if her tugs on her nipples were pulling her body off the bed.

And she moaned.

It sounded so fooking perfect.

Cam licked his own lips, his free hand instinctively dropping to the bulge in his trousers. *Nay, this is about her.*

"Spread yer legs," he rasped, and she complied.

With her heels against the counterpane, she spread her knees, lifting her arse off the bed, allotting him the most beautiful view of her cunny, already glistening with need.

Unable to help himself, he closed his fingers around the front of his trousers, his cock aching to spring free.

He swallowed, remembering the way those inner lips tasted, remembering the way she'd come apart with his tongue inside her. "Touch yerself," he commanded. "Drag yer finger along yer folds. I want to see it."

She didn't hesitate to obey.

With one hand still fondling her tit, Jade dropped the other to her curls. One long, slender finger dipped into her wet core, then dragged upward, toward her clitoris.

They both sucked in a breath when she reached it, when she brushed against it once, twice. The pad of her finger worked the bud, and she let out a little whimper, which caused his fingers to tighten instinctively around his cock.

God Almighty, he wanted to stroke himself. Nay, he wanted to cross the room, to lean over her, to place his mouth where her fingers were, to plunge into her again and again.

But he wouldn't.

"That's it, Treasure," he choked, his gaze riveted to the sight of that finger, dipping in and out of her curls. "Are ye imagining my hands on ye?"

"Your lips," she groaned. "Kissing me here and here." A second finger joined the first. "Your fingers, stroking me into —" She broke off with another moan.

He made a little noise of approval, which caused her to whimper. Her back arched again, and she took her tit full in her hand and *squeezed.*

"Wider," he ordered, forcing his voice to work. "Spread yer legs wider." He waited until she complied. "Now use both hands. Touch yer beautiful cunny for me, Jade."

She slid her palms down her stomach to her curls, then down the insides of her thighs and back, as if she were teasing both of them. With her thumb and forefinger of each hand, she spread her outer lips, putting herself on display for him.

The glistening evidence of her arousal was plain, and Cam ached to be inside her. "Where do ye want me?"

"Here," she immediately answered, her eyes closed and her head thrown back. "I want your fingers here." She stroked herself. "I want them inside me."

"Can ye feel yer pleasure mounting, lass?" The side of his fingers rubbed at his own arousal. "Building inside ye, ready to break free?"

"Yes!" she gasped. "Cam, please!"

"Push yer fingers inside yerself, Treasure," he demanded. "Like ye do when ye're alone at night. Except now, I'm watching."

She hesitated, her eyes flying open as she met his gaze. He saw her swallow, saw her legs quiver with desire, and then... she obeyed him.

As he watched, she pushed first one, then two fingers into her slick core, curling them instinctively upward and toward her, so she could press the base of her palm where the pressure was building.

"Does that feel good?" he murmured.

She whimpered and dropped her head back again. "*So* good."

"Slide them out again. Now...in."

She obeyed, this time using her third and fourth fingers, so she could hold her lips spread with the outer digits. The other hand rose and began to tease her clitoris, and she moaned again, a breathless little whimper Cam knew he'd never tire of.

He realized he was holding his own breath, and forced himself to inhale. With her eyes closed, it appeared she was in her own world, and he resisted the urge to pleasure himself. Nay, he wanted to watch this, to enjoy this, so later... Later, he could remember this. Remember *her*.

Her movements grew more frantic, as she played with her bud and finger-fooked herself. She was approaching her orgasm.

"Ye're close, Treasure." It wasn't a question. He could see the evidence in the way her muscles strained, in the dripping arousal clinging to her fingers. "So close. Do ye want to come?"

"Yes! Please!" she groaned, her fingers working frantically in and out.

"Do it," he growled. "Come for me."

With a moan that turned into a keen, Jade's arse clenched, her thighs tightened, and he watched as she froze, her fingers deep inside her. Slowly, her knees closed, trapping her hand between her legs.

Panting now, she rolled to one side, her fingers still trapped inside her, and when she began to thrust against her own touch, Cam cursed silently, his own fingers tightening around his desperate cock.

She was curled on the bed, fooking her own fingers, at *his* command. And he could do nothing more than watch.

Finally, with a heaving gasp, Jade wrenched her hands away from herself and flopped, boneless, against the mattress. She was breathing heavily, and Cam saw moisture at the corners of her closed eyes.

Ye did that.

Ye did that to her.

Nay, *for* her. Right?

With another silent curse, Cam made himself loosen his white-knuckled grip on the doorframe, made himself turn away.

Aye, he was running. But he *had* to…or they'd both regret the outcome.

THAT WAS…

Exhilarating.

Wonderful.

Empowering.

Embarrassing as hell.

Wait, what?

Look at you, splayed out like some kind of banquet. He didn't once touch you.

He didn't need to. She'd found ecstasy all on her own.

It could've been better.

Yes, if he'd been a part of it.

But…he'd stood on the other side of the room, he'd watched her. He'd ordered her—and she'd obeyed! He'd said such wonderfully erotic things...and she'd experienced an orgasm to rival the ones he'd given her that first night.

And he hadn't even touched her.

That realization made her feel perversely proud *and* achingly hollow at the same time.

Suddenly cold, whereas moments ago she'd been so very hot, Jade pulled her knees to her chest, and wondered if it was possible to forget the last few minutes. Wondered if she wanted to.

Get up. Go to him.

She wasn't one to shy away from a problem, or a mystery. She needed to understand Cam MacKay...especially in relation to what had just happened.

So she forced herself upright, shaking her hands to will some life back into her limbs, which still felt a gentle buzzing. She washed in the warm water he'd brought for her, and dressed in the only gown she'd brought along for this trip.

It was a pale blue, one of her favorites, and she thought it did nice things for the odd color of her eyes. When she'd planned for this journey, she'd assumed she'd be here for no more than a day or two, and had packed accordingly. With just the two of them in The Cottage, she hadn't felt ashamed to be wearing the same skirt and rotating her simple blouses, the ones she wore to her office.

It was strange, to be so comfortable so far away from London and her company. She had handpicked the men who were overseeing Thacker Shipping in her absence, and she wasn't uncomfortable knowing they were in charge. She hadn't told them how long she'd be gone, so they likely weren't worried...and she had to admit the last few days had been relaxing.

Because of *him*.

Cam, who'd made her come apart, without even touching her.

That was why now, she wanted to feel powerful. So she donned the gown, and pulled her hair back in the simple tail she wore when she visited the fencing club. It wasn't a flattering style, but it was easy to accomplish alone, and she needed to hurry.

To see him.

Still, by the time she stepped into the parlor, he'd obviously found time to change as well. He was fully dressed—which was a shame, because she would've liked the chance to stare at his chest some more, even if most of it had been covered by that towel he'd draped around his shoulders before he'd come into her room. He stood with his back to her in front of one of the windows, facing the sea.

The rain had started up again, pounding at the panes of glass with a vengeance, which made her glad they'd ventured outside when they had. And not because of the kiss.

Well, fine, not *just* because of the kiss.

Perhaps she made some noise, because he turned. His curls were still damp, and he held a glass in his hand—brandy, she guessed. He seemed partial to the sweet drink. Her eyes darted to the side, and sure enough, a small plate with the last of yesterday's cookies rested on the table.

Cam shifted his weight, as if unsure what to say, then jerked his chin toward the window. "The storm returned."

"Yes," she said awkwardly, hovering in the doorway.

He cleared his throat, then turned back to the view. "The window is beginning to leak. I'm worried."

A safe subject, at least. "Where?" She hurried across the room, and he pointed to where the glass met the frame.

"All through here, and across the top, see? The window is much older than the thatch—I just had that redone—and I suppose the constant pounding from the wind offshore is causing it to weaken."

Humming, Jade dragged her finger through the puddle of

water which had collected. "I admit, I expected the thatch to give way before this onslaught…"

Scoffing good-naturedly, Cam shook his head and gestured with the brandy. "This is fine Scottish thatch, Miss Thacker. It will stand up to a wee breeze."

Her smile was almost shy. "Bracing sea air, hmm?"

"Aye." He stilled, staring down at her, his knuckles white around his glass.

She wondered what he was thinking. Wondered if he was fighting the urge to touch her, as she was him.

She had to know.

Blowing out a breath, she lifted her chin and met his eyes. "Cam, why did you not come to me?"

He jerked forward, but didn't reach for her. Instead he swallowed and looked away.

She didn't want to hear his denial. "In the bedroom. I wanted you. I wanted you to be with me. But…"

Was this shame? This warm feeling fading through her limbs? She wasn't certain. She reached out and touched his arm, but he jerked back.

Yes, definitely shame.

"Cam?" she asked again, her throat choked with hurt.

Without looking at her, he turned, slammed the brandy down on the table beside the cookies, and stalked toward the center of the room. "What do ye want me to say, Treasure?" The words burst out of him in frustration as he dragged his hands through his hair. "Ye want me to tell ye how badly I wanted to climb onto that bed with ye, to taste ye?"

He still wasn't looking at her, so she felt safe whispering, "Yes."

He blew out a breath, tugging at his curls. "Well, it's true. Hardest fooking thing I've done, keeping my hands to myself today." His arms dropped to his sides, his chin sunk to his chest. "And yesterday. And the day before."

The admission sent a jolt of *something*—pride? Excitement? —through her, but she hesitated to go to him. Instead, she crossed to the sofa where he'd been sleeping, and perched on the edge of the cushion.

"Why, Cam? I thought ye were..." She swallowed, not certain how to form the words.

"A whore?" He huffed mirthlessly, staring down at the small blaze he'd started in the hearth. "A courtesan. A rake."

Well... "A lover," she whispered.

Suddenly, he whirled, one finger outstretched accusingly. "Ye dinnae want to be married, remember, Jade? But we *are*, and as soon as it's safe to travel, ye and I are getting on a train to MacKay lands to confront my father, aye?"

She nodded, her hands held stiffly in her lap. "I'd like to know the truth."

"Aye, and if we *are* married, then it was against yer will, and an annulment will be easy enough to obtain." A tortured look came to his eyes as he crossed to the sofa, sinking down beside her. "I'll tell the judge the truth, Jade, dinnae doubt it. Ye'll no' have to stay married to the likes of me for verra long."

The likes of me.

Ai-ya, did the man not realize how wonderful he was?

With a soft smile, Jade reached for his hands, then scooted closer so she could clasp them in her lap as she held his gaze.

"And you think making love to me would make the annulment harder to obtain?"

He immediately nodded. "I'll say whatever is necessary, Treasure. I'm sorry my father's put ye in this situation, but ye'll no' have to endure it long, I swear."

"He put *you* in this situation too, Cam."

He glanced away, his attention fixed unconvincingly on the flames. "I find I dinnae mind it so much," he finally admitted.

And neither, to her surprise, did she.

Of course, it was difficult, not knowing what was going on

back in London with Thacker Shipping. But she had her managers and her assistants, all of whom knew where she was, in case of an emergency. And if there *was* an emergency, at least the company had the capital now to handle it, thanks to the partner she'd taken on.

She took a deep breath and squeezed his hands. "What I said to you that night in the hotel…I was there because I was tired of feeling powerless. I want to use the money *Gung Gung* left me to grow Thacker Shipping. But if I'm married before my birthday—to a man who forces the issue, or to someone my uncle chooses—my husband will control that money."

"Ye…" He swallowed. "Ye had to take on a silent partner."

Oh yes, she'd told him that, hadn't she?

"I hate that I'm not in complete control, so I plan to buy the man out as soon as I gain the rest of my inheritance, and my lawyers find out his name. But in the meantime…" She quirked a wry smile and squeezed his hands. "Lord Buthert was becoming a nuisance, arriving at my office daily, surprising me at home, cornering me on the street. I was genuinely terrified he was going to try something, something which would force me to marry him before my birthday, so he would gain my inheritance."

"Buthert? I hate to say it, lass, but I can absolutely imagine him doing that."

Of course Cam knew him. Buthert had been at the club the day she'd sparred with Cam, and had called out that rude comment about Cam's concentration. But the fact he knew Buthert meant his opinion was likely right. "Yes, I don't think it was so far-fetched as a fear. But…" She blew out a breath. "I'm making a mess of this explanation."

"Keep trying, lass."

And she could tell, from his sincere expression, that he meant it. So she took a deep breath and tried again.

"I don't object to marriage, Cam, as long as it is *my* decision. But that money was left to me, and I intend to use it to keep my father's company—*my* company—running strong. Then your father began to hint at a marriage between me and you—a man I only knew from his letters—to solve my problems, and I felt so…"

"Trapped," he murmured.

She met his eyes. "That night, you gave me power. You gave it *back* to me. I needed that. But you also…" She struggled to explain. "You did something to me. Since then, I haven't been able to…" She shook her head. "You changed me," she repeated.

"And today?" He quirked a brow at her.

It was impossible to know if he'd understood her, but she smiled. "Yes, today was wonderful, again. Thank you."

"God Almighty," he muttered, slumping. "I've turned ye insatiable."

Her sudden peal of laughter took her by surprise, and she flopped back beside him. "Yes, I suppose you have." She took a deep breath and twined her fingers through his "My point is, I like to be in control of my life. I hated that Lord Buthert was trying to force me into a situation I couldn't control, and then to have your uncle do the same…"

As she shook her head, he squeezed her fingers.

"Ye'll no' have to stay married to a man like me, Treasure," he vowed. "Or Buthert."

Was he putting himself in the same category as that snake? "Buthert is a vile opportunist who'll stop at nothing to get what he wants."

"Aye, a sack of diseased cow shite."

She cocked a brow at Cam. "How well do you know him?"

He shrugged. "I wouldn't trust him to back down, no matter what obstacles you put in his way."

"Yes," she sighed. "That was your father's thinking as well. Hence the marriage suggestion."

"Hence the marriage by proxy," Cam corrected.

She turned her head so her cheek was pressed against the hard back of the sofa, and she was staring at him. "Yes," she murmured softly. "But as you say, it isn't so bad."

His gaze was on her lips. "Nay," he whispered, leaning forward almost unconsciously. "Much better than a life as Lady Buthert."

Her lips curled. "True." She held her breath, hoping he was going to kiss her.

That's when the glass panes surrendered to the force of the storm, and the window blew in.

CHAPTER 8

THE PAINTED CANVAS from that twisty game came in handy after all; while Jade held it against the broken frame, Cam attached it with some nails and a hammer he found in one of the cabinets.

It wasn't perfect, but it did a respectable job of keeping the wind out, although the parlor became much darker almost immediately. The rain had pooled under the window, and as more soaked the canvas, they knew their makeshift measure wouldn't keep the room dry.

"I'll get pots," Jade volunteered, rolling up her damp sleeves as she headed toward the kitchen.

"And I'll start on the pane." Cam scooped up the waste basket, then lowered himself to his haunches to begin carefully retrieving as much of the broken glass as possible so it wouldn't cut either of them.

After a few frantic minutes of activity, the pair of them sat back on their heels and looked around. Jade blew out a breath at the same time he began to chuckle. When she raised a brow at him, he shrugged.

"The Cottage is small enough, and with this chill, I'm guessing our time using this room is at an end."

Humming, she glanced around the room and seemed to come to some conclusion. She pushed herself to her feet, and offered him her hand. "Then let us see what we can do about salvaging the furnishings before they become moister, eh?"

He winced.

"What?"

Teasingly, he brushed his hands on his trousers, then accepted her hand. He didn't need her help, but it was nice to allow her to pretend she was lifting him. After what they'd just shared—not what he'd said and seen and done in the bedroom, but what they'd *shared* here moments ago—he didn't mind letting her issue commands.

But Jade held his hand longer than was necessary. "You don't think we need to bother moving these things?" She was referring to his wince.

"Nay, lass, I agree, it would be best to save them. It was yer use of 'moister' I was objecting to."

One black brow rose in challenge. "It's a word."

"Aye, but…" He grinned wryly. "Nae one likes the word 'moist'. If ye were to take the umbrella and tromp into the village, and ask around the pub, not a single man there—nor the women who take rooms upstairs—would tell ye they like the word moist. None of them. And *moister* is even worse."

She pretended to gasp. "I think I'm offended on behalf of the word. *Moist.* Moist, moister, moistest." When Cam winced theatrically again, she smacked his shoulder. "Surely there are worse words? I've never cared for 'curd'. Or 'squid'."

"*Ointment*," he volunteered, still grinning. "*Bulbous.*"

It was obvious she was fighting a smile. "Phlegm. Lugubrious?"

"Fester! *Squirt.*"

One of Jade's fingers poked him in the chest. "There. Now

those words are terrible. Likely because of the subject matter. 'Moist' is perfectly fine."

"Ye're still saying it!"

"What other words convey the same meaning? Damp? Dank, clammy, muggy? I'd rather put a moist chocolate cake in my mouth, than a dank and clammy one!" She poked him again. "Moist is a—"

He caught her finger before she could poke him a third time. "Treasure," he asked in a mock-serious tone, "what do I need to do to get you to stop saying mo—*that* word?"

She grinned. "Help me move furniture."

Of course he was happy to let her take the lead, as she began barking orders and plans for the furnishings. And he was happy to lend his strength to the task, knowing the burn in his muscles was what he needed to distract himself from the intimacy of the day.

Not just how she'd looked, spread out on his bed, finger-fooking herself. But the way she'd held his hand as they'd sat in the parlor, talking about...*everything.*

It took them the rest of the day, but by the evening, most of the furniture and books from the parlor had been moved into one of the empty bedchambers. The contents of the cabinets were deemed by Jade to be safe from damp, so they remained.

The only exceptions were the large sofa he'd been sleeping on, which couldn't fit through the parlor door without three more burly men, and the chaise and leather chair—along with a small table—she'd instructed him to move into the dining room.

Once there, she had him shift the dining table to one side—storing all but two of the chairs along one wall—and set about arranging the new furniture in front of the hearth. By the time she was finished, the dining room now boasted a much smaller dining area, but a cozy little sitting area to take the place of their inoperable parlor.

They were too tired to attempt anything out of the recipe book, so with the rain still beating down upon the thatch, they enjoyed simple sandwiches and some sliced apples from earlier in the season.

There was a concern which had been tickling the back of Cam's mind since they realized the sofa would have to stay in the parlor. He was hoping to find an extra blanket to keep himself warm tonight, and wished he had his great coat to sleep in.

But Jade surprised him—of course she did—by taking his hand after they finished cleaning up from dinner. Her smile seemed...hesitant. It wasn't an expression he was used to seeing on this maybe-wife's face.

"Cam, you cannot sleep on the sofa."

He dismissed her with a wry grin. "Of course I can. A little cold and damp never killed anyone."

One elegant brow rose. "First of all, yes, *plenty* of people are killed by being chilled and moist."

Since he was certain she'd chosen that word just to rile him, he winced dramatically again.

"And second of all," she continued, "it is foolish to tempt fate when you *do* have access to a bed. A *large* bed, big enough for both of us."

Cam stifled his sigh, knowing he wouldn't be strong enough to resist her if she persisted. "Treasure," he murmured, lifting his palm to her cheek. "I cannae. Ye ken that."

"I promise to keep my hands to myself." Her gray eyes were pleading as she tipped her head back to meet his gaze. "Please, Cam? I will feel far too guilty to sleep if you're not warm and comfortable tonight, too."

Well, fook. There was no escaping her sweet *please*, was there?

Och, dinnae pretend to be a martyr. Ye'd cut off yer left nut to be able to sleep beside her!

Well, perhaps not his left *nut*.

But aye, it didn't take much convincing for him to give in, to follow her back to the bedroom, to each perform their ablutions in private, then slip into the large, warm bed.

And there *was* enough space for them to sleep without touching, but somehow, Jade's cheek found its way to his shoulder, and his arm found its way around her waist.

She drooled a bit.

It was adorable.

If Cam hadn't been falling in love with her already, that night, holding her in his arms, would've cinched it. He woke up curled around her, and knew it was the best night's sleep he'd achieved since he'd arrived.

The raging cockstand was almost worth it.

Luckily, he rolled out of bed before Jade could notice—or comment—on it, and padded barefoot, in just the shirt and trousers he'd slept in, to the kitchen to start boiling water for the day.

It was a...*cozy* sort of existence, this interlude at The Cottage. The pair of them, working together, teasing each other, reading or playing silly games in their new sitting area in the dining room. He still hadn't had the chance to dig through the reports from last quarter, but they could wait.

Everything could wait; his investments, his father, the outside world. As far as Cam was concerned, this rain could last for forty days and nights, until the rest of the world—including London—was swept away, leaving only him and Jade alone. Together.

But all good things must come to an end.

And truthfully, he didn't *want* London to be swept away in The Next Great Flood. He liked the pastry chefs there. And his tailor. And that one coffee shop where the hostess always flirted with him and gave him an extra sweet bun. Aye, he'd miss parts of the city.

Even if he wasn't ready to return.

On the morning of their eighth day at The Cottage, Cam woke on his side, cradling Jade in his arms. Her sweet little arse was pressed up against his cock, which nestled perfectly along the cleft he could feel beneath her nightgown. God Almighty, but it was the most perfect torture, was it not?

One of his arms was tucked under the pillow, the other was thrown across her side, resting on her stomach.

And her hand rested on top of it, her slim fingers wrapped around his.

Almost as if, in sleep, she *did* want him.

Dinnae get a big head, laddie. Nae one else has ever wanted ye. Why should she?

True. But Cam had never wanted anyone else, either. Not the way he wanted this woman in his arms.

That's yer cock talking.

Nay—well, alright, *aye*. His cock wanted her. But he wanted her in other ways, too. He wanted to hold her, cherish her, show her that he was more than everyone assumed.

Gently, slowly, he turned his hand over in her hold, so their fingers were still entwined, but their palms pressed against each other.

In the silence of dawn, Cam marveled at the feel of her hand in his, her body pressed so trustingly against his, and listened to the sound of her breathing.

It took a while to realize that was the *only* sound he heard.

The rain had stopped.

Frowning, he rolled away, taking her hand with him. She murmured happily and rolled as well, pressing herself against him. Lying on his back, he listened to the sound of the wind, and realized the storm had finally blown itself out, although the weather was likely still raw and damp outside.

No' moist. Never moist.

Unconsciously, his thumb was rubbing small circles on her

palm. His second hand joined the first, and his lips twitched at the lazy comfort of it, just touching her. Just exploring her.

The pads of his fingers found a callus on her index finger, and he traced it carefully. From writing, no doubt. She was an industrious, admirable businesswoman.

But…something about the callus was familiar. Cam could never be called a good student, not in the same way Malcolm was, and *he* had this same callus. A long one, along the edge of his index finger. It didn't come from holding a pen, but from holding a…

Holding a sword.

Curious now, Cam pushed himself upright, peering down at her hand in the poor light. Sure enough, her finger bore the same callus his did, in miniature.

Why would she be holding a sword?

Jade stirred, and when he glanced at her, she was smiling sleepily up at him. "Good morning, Cam."

And he had to fight the urge to bend down and kiss her, knowing that something so simple could hurt him beyond doubt. When she walked away.

But still, he forced a smile, and curled his hands around hers once more. "Good morning, Treasure. The rain's stopped."

She cocked her head to one side, and nodded. "I believe you're— "A yawn interrupted her, and he had to chuckle.

"Come along. Let us break our fast and go out to investigate the damage."

The Cottage had survived the deluge well enough. Besides the wrecked parlor window, a good amount of the thatch had been damaged, although there were no leaks yet. Cam made a note to inquire with his usual thatchers in the village, and have them come investigate.

Otherwise, the main problem was the mud.

"This is ridiculous!" Jade called out, laughter in her voice, as she bent to untie her boot. "I'm going to lose these one way or the other, so it might as well be of my own volition!"

And that was how the pair of them spent the day barefoot —her skirt tucked up high enough to give him intriguing views of her calves, his kilt already mud-spattered—fixing up what they could under a threatening sky full of fast-moving gray clouds.

In the afternoon, Cam took her down to the beach, where he was reminded yet again of how remarkable she truly was. She identified any number of strange sea creatures which had been washed up by the storm, and even followed him gamely into one of the sea caves.

A squall blew through, sending them running back to shelter, breathless from laughter. Cam could tell from the smell of the air that it would be short. Assuming the sun came out tomorrow, and the roads dried a bit, he and Jade could make their way to the train station sooner than he wanted.

Aye, their interlude would be over tomorrow, one way or the other.

But there was something he was curious about, first.

So after they got cleaned up—she refused to let him boil enough water for a bath, claiming with a laugh that she didn't need it—he met her in the foyer. After wracking his brain, he still couldn't come up with a nonchalant way to bring up her callus, so he decided to be direct.

By handing her a furled umbrella.

"What's this?" she asked, frowning down at it.

Feeling ten times a fool, and glad no one was there to witness it except her, Cam lifted the remaining umbrella in an *en guard* position, one hand held behind him.

Her brows went up.

"Cam? Are you feeling well?"

"Aye. I just feel the need for some exercise."

Her knuckles had tightened around the umbrella's shaft.

"We spent all day out of doors. Do you want to go on another walk in the rain?"

"Nay." He took a deep breath and raised his "foil". "I want ye to defend yerself."

She opened her mouth—likely to ask him what in the name of Christ and the little fishes he was *doing*—but he didn't give her the opportunity.

He lunged.

And as he expected, she parried.

"Cam! What are you doing?"

"Fencing!" He lunged again, and she parried again. "I expected ye to be better!"

He suspected Jade Thacker didn't do *anything* without becoming very good at it.

"Did you?" She knocked aside another attack, then a fourth. This time, she twisted under his guard, the tip of her umbrella slid perilously close to his ribs before he could knock it aside. "You are right, of course."

Laughter burst from his lips, as she went on the offensive. He was right; she *was* good, and her style was somehow familiar. Definitely similar to his, at least.

"Where did ye train?" His back foot bumped against the door, telling him it was time to stop giving ground and push *her* back. "Ye have remarkable balance."

She acknowledged the compliment with a flourish of her umbrella, and a small smile. "My father taught me, along with his sailing master. Later, he hired a training master, although I found it difficult to find bouts."

"Nonsense." Cam was delighted to discover he was short of breath. He'd missed this play, this banter, this give and take on the strip. Even the foyer of The Cottage was worth it. "There are circuits of women's fencing bouts, are there no'? The papers publish sketches of their outlandish wear—"

Jade's "*Ha!*" was accompanied by a point, proving he'd been too distracted. She stepped back, settling into guard with a smug smile. "Have you ever *seen* a women's match? Some of them are quite skilled, but there's no fervor, no desperation."

"Ah," he drawled thoughtfully, before lunging. "So ye want blood?"

"No," she panted, parrying with a grin. "I want to fight an opponent who wants blood."

His laughter distracted him again, and she darted in for another point. He blocked and twisted in time, and decided it was time to show her *his* skills.

The hall was silent but for their heavy breathing and the clash of their makeshift foils. Then, she surprised him.

With a quiet grunt, Jade swung the umbrella in from the side, catching him unprepared.

"Another point!" she whooped, dropping back into guard position with a triumphant smile.

He scowled, rubbing his bruised hip. "That didnae count. It was below my waist, *and* ye swung…instead of…lunging." His eyes narrowed as he remembered another opponent who'd surprised him similarly. "Have ye fenced with a backsword?"

"No, a saber," she chirped. "I was raised among sailors, remember! And I thought ye had training with the *claidheamh?*"

"Aye, I used to—" His teeth snapped together as he realized what she'd said, and he dropped his arm. "It *was* ye! That afternoon at the club!" Tossing the umbrella aside, he stalked toward her. "Ye were my opponent, the Chinaman?"

She was watching his face, and as he approached, shuffled back two steps. But she seemed to catch herself, realizing she was running. Her chin came up, her shoulders straightened, and she lowered her umbrella a moment before he reached her.

Her light hold on the makeshift foil allowed him to wrench

it from her hand. His fingers closed around her wrist as he lifted her hand so he could examine the tell-tale callus.

"Ye *are* a fencer," he muttered, switching his gaze to her face.

She was chewing on her lower lip when she nodded, as if she didn't know what to expect from him. He blew out a breath and shook his head.

"Damnation, Treasure, ye really *are* remarkable." Under his fingers, her pulse jumped. "That really was ye? That day at my club?"

"I didn't know it was you," she whispered. "Not until you removed your mask."

His thumb pressed against her inner wrist as he huffed slightly. "I remember ye scurried off after that." He'd been distracted by Da's letter, but he *had* noted "the Chinaman's" disappearance.

"Well, you would have as well." Her chin jutted out mulishly. "If you'd realized you'd been beaten by the man you'd just given your virginity to."

His grin was crooked when he laid his other hand on her hip, drawing her closer and trapping her wrist between them. "I gave it back to ye, if ye'll recall," he murmured, staring down at her. "And it seems a shame now, to ken these curves were hidden beneath that costume."

"Curves?" She snorted, but didn't pull away. "I'm *straight*. And it's just a man's fencing suit. I barely had to wrap my breasts, since the canvas is so stiff."

With his hand holding hers against his chest, it was easy enough to brush the edge of two fingers along the tops of her breasts, smiling as she swallowed a shiver.

"As I said, a shame," he repeated. "But how did ye talk them into allowing ye to spar? And why did ye no' tell me?"

She sighed. "Money can buy rather a lot of privilege, Cam. And as for the second..." She shook her head, dropping her gaze to his chin. "I suppose I didn't see a need for it. You hadn't asked, and the manager of the club told me he'd immediately rescind my membership if there was ever a whisper of my name in association—"

"Ye're a club *member*?"

Her smile seemed a bit sad. "Bribery is a tool a successful businesswoman must use often. I am only allowed inside if I sneak in through the servants' entrance dressed as a maid, and change in a private room." She shrugged. "But it's the only place in London where I can find a proper bout."

He remembered. "An opponent who wants blood."

"An opponent who is serious about winning," she corrected.

A thought struck him, and he instinctively tightened his hold on her, pulling her closer. "Ye...dinnae mind I ken?" His eyes flicked between hers, reassuring himself. "Ye said ye told nae one, but—"

Her free hand snaked around his back and she tilted her head back to hold his gaze. "I trust you, Cam. I never meant to keep it a secret from you, not really. And your feelings matter more to me than my spot in the club, anyhow."

As if his mind—and his heart—wasn't reeling from such a casual confession, Jade shrugged. "I don't like secrets."

And just like that, his budding euphoria jerked backward, a guilty pit opening in his stomach. "I dinnae—dinnae like secrets either." Damnation, that stumble made him sound guilty.

So did the way she rolled her eyes.

"You don't like secrets? You're keeping a big one, aren't you?"

Ah.

Talking about secrets was fine when it was *her* secret. But he shifted uneasily, releasing her hand, but unwilling to release her entirely.

"Like what?" he hedged.

Her finger poked him in the chest. "Like you not keeping my money!" When he tried to protest, she cut him off with an angry-sounding, "*Ai-ya!* You let it slip our first day here in The Cottage! I paid you to show me pleasure, and you didn't keep my money." Another poke. "What happened to it, Cam? What did you do with it?"

He tried for a grin as he loosened his hold and stepped back from her, trying not to wince as her hand fell away from him. "I spent it."

"No, you didn't!"

And that's when he realized she wasn't angry-*sounding*. She was *angry*. He frowned, trying to understand her pique.

"It was my money, lass. Ye gave it to me."

"And you gave it away, didn't you?"

Why was this important? He shrugged again, suddenly feeling foolish to be having this conversation in the foyer, the umbrellas standing ready to tangle in his feet. "So what if I did? Why does it matter to ye—"

"Because that's the *real you*!"

He shook his head and planted his hands on his hips, pleased he hadn't bothered with a jacket after all. "I dinnae understand why this is important."

Jade blew out a heavy breath and pinched the bridge of her nose, her eyes squeezed shut. "No, I don't suppose I'm explaining myself very well, am I?" She inhaled, then shook her head, eyes still closed. "Cam, you try so hard to be a rake. A simple man, a *lazy* man, interested in one thing."

"Nay, I—"

Her hand dropped to her hips in a matching pose and she suddenly pierced him with a fierce glare. "You are perfectly happy to allow Society to think you a—a—*philanderer*, a dim-witted socialite who is more handsome than most, and whose sole goal is pleasure—his and women's."

His lips curled wryly. "Ye think I'm handsomer than most?"

"*Focus*, Cam!" But her lips twitched in response, and she blew out a breath. "You're more than that. You care, you protect, and you're smart and funny and interesting. But you pretend not to be." She held his gaze. "Why?"

Well, *fook*.

She wasn't going to back down, was she?

Jade raised a brow. "I'm not going to back down."

Double fook.

CHAPTER 9

SHE COULD TELL from his expression that he was trying to find a way to lie to her. Well, not *lie* exactly, but... Jade sighed. Cam had a tendency to deflect serious topics, or things he didn't want to discuss, with a flirtatious comment or gorgeous, dimply smile.

She wasn't going to fall for it, this time. And she wasn't going to let him get away without answering.

"Cam..." She lowered her voice and took a step nearer to him, holding her arms out. "What is it?"

He didn't respond, but when she wrapped her arms around his middle and pressed her cheek against his shoulder, he didn't pull away. True, he was stiffer than week-old bread, his arms held awkwardly at his sides, but he allowed the embrace.

"Why do you hide who you really are?" she murmured against him.

Slowly, so slowly she might've imagined it, she felt him relax. He exhaled, each moment leeching more of his rigidity, his uncharacteristic severity, from him.

"Cam?" she prompted, tilting her head back to peer up at him, her hands locked behind him.

His own head was tilted back, so he was staring up at the ceiling. Still, she saw a flicker of a wince cross his face.

"My family," he finally confessed. "*Families.*"

There was something...*hollow* in his admission. She squeezed. "They're the reason you hide your true self?"

He sighed, then lifted his hand to scrub across his face, without touching her. From behind his palm, he admitted, "I've always been an inconvenience to my mother, and her husband has never had a use for me. And my father was..."

Suddenly, it all clicked into place in her mind. She waited for him to finish, and when he didn't, she gently did it for him. "Your father used to be a rake and a charmer, didn't he? So you were following in his footsteps."

He dropped his hand slowly, tipping his head down to meet her eyes. After a long moment, the confusion in his gaze turned to acceptance. "Aye, that's it. I suppose I wanted him to notice me."

"So you became who you thought he would notice." That made sense, in a round-about way. "Did he tell you otherwise?"

With a sigh, Cam wrapped his own arms around her. "He's no' a bad man, ye ken, other than this high-handed marriage by proxy. He cares deeply, and wants to do what's right—"

The parallels were obvious. "Like you?"

"Look, can we have this conversation some other time?"

She smirked, knowing it was hidden against his chest. "Not at all. I'm enjoying myself."

"My feet hurt."

"You're the idiot who fences barefoot."

He smiled, then shifted. "Can we sit down, at least?"

She squeezed again. "I'll let you sit if you tell me why you think your father would like you better as a rake."

"I *dinnae.*" He sighed again, then planted his chin atop her head. "He loves me, but as he settled down—he didnae marry yer aunt until I was already off at school, ye ken—he started to change. For the better, I assume. But I didnae realize that until I was the darling of Society."

Snorting softly, she moved her head out from under him. "Darling of Society? You think highly of yourself."

Instead of returning her banter, he chuckled. "I suppose...it was easy to fall into that role, especially since it was expected of me. Being one of the Kilted Bastards, and all that. And..." He shrugged. "It was what my mother and her husband expected. They said I was lazy, and good for nothing besides hedonism."

"So you embraced it."

"It's easier than fighting what they think of me, but I ken the truth. I proved them wrong." His voice dropped, and she wasn't certain he was still speaking to her when he repeated, "They didnae want me, and they're no' worth the trouble of proving they're wrong about me."

Her heart ached for him. "But you know," she whispered.

His, "But I ken," was barely audible.

She peeked up at him, to see his eyes shut. "And now I do too." She knew the truth about him.

"What?" His eyes flashed open, and he frowned in confusion.

"I know they're wrong about you. *Everyone's* wrong about you."

His blue gaze caressed her face. "Except ye?"

"Except me," she agreed.

"Can we sit down *now*? All this lovey-dovey shite and emotional rawness is making my feet hurt more."

She couldn't help it; she began to giggle. Pulling away from him, she twined her fingers through his and pulled him toward the dining room and their improvised little sitting area.

"So...a courtesan who doesn't keep his earnings, a remarkably gifted fencer, the best kisser Society has ever known, and a whiner." She threw him a cheeky grin as she tugged him down to the small chaise. "The whiniest whiner who ever whined—"

"Ye think I'm a good kisser?"

Her grin growing, Jade tucked her feet up under her rear end and turned to face him. This close, she could see something in his eyes which looked like uncertainty. Uncertainty from *this* man was nearly heartbreaking.

"I know it, remember?" she murmured, laying her palm against his cheek. "You're a brilliant kisser, and a good man, Cam. So tell me what you did with that money."

"God Almighty, Jade!" The words burst out of him with a heavy breath, and he fell back against the chaise. "Ye're no' going to let this go, are ye?"

Still smiling, she rested her elbow beside his head, propped up her chin on her fist, and leaned closer. "I'm no' going to let this go," she repeated breezily. "You might as well tell me. I don't like mysteries."

"I'm no' a mystery."

"You are." She dropped a quick kiss to the corner of his mouth she could reach, then sat up again. "Beautiful, kind, caring, sweet, and keeping secrets."

His eyes were closed, but she could see a muscle in his jaw working as the silence lengthened. Was he contemplating what to tell her?

Finally he exhaled softly. "The Saving Grace and the Rest of Them as Well charity orphanage. I dropped the whole wallet in their collection box."

He'd surprised her. "That was…a ridiculous amount of money, Cam." Her eyes were wide.

He winced. "I dinnae always donate to them. Sometimes to other orphanages, sometimes…" He shook his head. "There are plenty of good causes which need money more than I do."

The part of her which had managed her father's empire for so long, the part which had sat on his knee and learned the ins and outs of business, was still in shock. "You *worked* for that money, Cam! It was payment—"

When he sat up, turning a glare on her, her lips pressed together.

"I didnae *work* for it, Treasure, remember? Ye did the work."

"Well, yes, *that* instance. But I came to you with a purpose, and you gave me what I asked for, and I paid you for it. That's what *business* is! You're a courtesan—"

A thought interrupted her so suddenly, she gasped aloud. A spasm of *something* crossed his face, and he turned away.

"You're *not* a courtesan, are you?" she whispered. "But Lady Melton told her sister, who told me, that you're the best in London. The ladies speak of you in hushed whispers, and your clients all brag…"

He scrubbed a hand over his face. "I'm no' a courtesan," he admitted. "I dinnae keep the money because I dinnae need it. And because…" He sighed, dropped his hand, and rolled his shoulders. "And because I dinnae fook."

"Ye dinnae…fook?"

"I give pleasure, Treasure." He turned back to her, looking more than a little defeated, and took her hands. "Just no' while fooking. My hands, my mouth, my words, sometimes…"

She shivered, remembering exactly how *much* pleasure he could give with his words, his hands, his mouth. "Yes," she whispered.

When he met her eyes, she couldn't read his gaze.

"Each of my clients kens what I'm willing to give them, and that's all they need. I never asked them to tell their friends differently, but I've heard the rumors too."

"But you do not…*fuck* them." *Ai-ya*, but the word felt satisfying on her tongue.

The way his lids lowered slightly told her he wasn't unaffected. "I dinnae."

"I don't understand."

His lips twitched. "My cock doesnae make acquaintance of their wet, dripping cunnies. I dinnae push my turgid sword into their quivering sheaths. I refrain from pounding my thick rod of love into their honeyed channels—"

Her giggles interrupted him, and she knocked her knuckles against his shoulders. "Honeyed channels? *Ai-ya,* that is dreadful! I *meant,* why do you not *make love* to these women? These clients?"

"Make love, hmm?" His fingers tightened around hers, and he took his time answering. "Because...I learned long ago when I *fook,* my heart becomes involved." He shrugged. "So I vowed only to fook when my heart *is* involved."

There was a story there. A deep, old pain, perhaps as old as the confessions he'd shared about his family. But Jade knew she'd hear it eventually.

Later.

In the future.

Because there *would* be a future for the two of them, she was certain now.

She knew what she wanted.

"Cam, you are...*remarkable.*"

He was shaking his head, ready to argue with her, as she lifted her leg and slid it across his thigh. His teeth clicked shut so quickly she thought she *heard* them. Or perhaps it was just his questioning hum as she shifted her weight, twisted slightly, and straddled him.

"Remarkable," she repeated in a whisper, settling against him. "You speak French, and know your Greek stems," she added, remembering his comments about *octopodes.* "You're smart, and kind—"

"French is the language of love," he interrupted.

"Stop trying to disparage yourself," she scolded as she scooched closer. "I know you."

Her thighs bracketed his, and she felt stretched. On display, despite being fully dressed.

His.

He, on the other hand, clearly didn't understand the implications. "Jade? What—"

She cupped his cheeks in her palms. "You hide this deep hurt, and determination, and high standards, and brilliant mind, and loving heart. You hide them under a mask of languor and laziness, because you don't want to challenge your family's perceptions of you."

His blue gaze, captured by her hands, raked her face. "Ye see me. The real me."

"I do."

Slowly, she leaned forward, taking his lips with hers.

It was a soft kiss, a slow kiss. Even as it deepened, Jade had the incredible feeling she was holding more than just his cheeks. She was holding his heart, and she knew how special that was.

His arms came up to wrap around her, settling against her buttocks, and she rocked forward. Although he didn't make a sound, she *felt* his sharp intake of breath at the same moment she registered the hard length of him trapped under his trousers.

It was likely cruel to rock against him again, teasing him, torturing herself. But *ai-ya!* She couldn't resist the sharp ache of *need* which pulsed through her.

Her tongue played lazily with his, and she didn't bother hiding her soft hums and mews and whimpers for *more more more.*

His fingers were digging into her rear end when she finally softened her lips and gently sat back. The movement pushed her pelvis against his once more, and he hissed softly, even as his gaze stroked her features.

"I love ye." He blinked, as if surprised.

Her eyes widened, and a satisfied grin tugged her lips upward. Before she could say anything, however, he pulled her closer.

"Nay, dinnae tell me I'm wrong, Treasure. I shouldnae have blurted it like a fool, but..." He reached up and carefully pulled her hands away from his cheeks, holding them between their bodies. "I love ye." He met her eyes. "These last days have showed me what I want in life."

Her heart was near pounding out of her rib cage, her pulse jumping about in victory. "What do you want in life?" she whispered, breathless.

"Ye, my treasure." Without dropping her gaze, he lifted first one hand, then the other, to his lips, brushing tantalizing kisses across her skin. "I want *ye*. I want companionship, and laughter, and someone to challenge me."

"At fencing?"

His lips curled into a grin. "At everything. I want—" He bit down on whatever he was about to admit, and his smile turned crooked. Charming.

Ai-ya, those dimples!

"I want ye to want me, Jade, as much as I want ye."

"Never doubt that." She twisted her fingers in his until she could touch his jaw. "Haven't you been paying attention to my not-very-subtle hints these last days?"

His grin turned wry. "Ye're insatiable."

She rocked forward again, her core—aching, pulsing, *moist* —cradling his hard length. "Only for you," she whispered boldly.

He groaned, his palm somehow finding its way to rest against the side of her neck. "God Almighty, lass, but ye're going to kill me."

"I'd like to fook you now, Cam."

"It'll be *making love*." His eyes met hers, and she felt a surge of victory when he finally confessed, "And I'd verra much like that too."

———

CAM SURRENDERED TO THE INEVITABLE.

Since that night in the hotel, since the moment his lips had claimed hers for the first time, since he'd watched her confidently fooking herself while he stroked his cock...he knew this would happen again.

He'd fought it. He'd tried to do the right thing, to be strong. But God knew he wanted this more than anything else he could imagine.

He wanted *her*.

She's an adult, and a brilliant one at that. She kens the reasons no' to do this.

So the fact she *did* want to do this...

Cam's subconscious likely had other things to say, other points to debate...but at that moment, Jade reached for the buttons of her high-necked blouse, and suddenly he couldn't form a single coherent thought.

He gave up arguing and reached to help her.

Undressing her seemed to take forever, in the most wonderful way. As the sky outside the window slowly darkened, and the logs popped and hissed in the hearth, he took his time stroking and kissing and nipping her flesh.

God Almighty, but this slow torture was everything he could've hoped for!

He was delighted to discover she hadn't bothered with her corset after she'd changed, which meant, once he pushed her blouse off her shoulders, the only thing standing between him and those delicious, dark nipples was a thin layer of cotton.

They were already stiff with anticipation, pebbling beneath his gaze.

He lowered his lips to her, pulling one into his mouth, teasing the peak as his tongue rasped against the wet cotton. With her arms trapped at her sides by her blouse, all she could do was tilt her head back and moan in encouragement.

Pulling away, he blew a gentle breath across her chemise, and could see small bumps rise across her chest as she shivered. The movement ground her pelvis against his, and his cock jumped in helpless anticipation.

Down, laddie, he warned himself.

Patience would be worth it. He was finally getting what he'd been longing for.

Longing for? Lust has addled ye.

Aye. His lips twitched as he switched their attention to the opposite nipple. He was addled, certainly. Addled for Miss Jade Thacker.

His possible wife.

Nay, after tonight: his *definite* wife.

No matter what Da confessed when they confronted him about the legality of this marriage by proxy.

Because Jade wanted this as much as Cam did, and he knew she knew what that meant.

After tonight, their future was sealed.

"Cam!" she gasped, her fingers digging into his hair. "*Ai-ya!*" She muttered something else in another language, and he chuckled around her nipple.

His hands stroked upward, tugging at the straps of her chemise, and he switched his kisses to her bare skin. "Do ye realize I cannae understand ye, Treasure?"

She groaned, grasping at his shoulders now, her breaths coming faster and faster. "I'll have to teach you—Oh! Yes, just like that."

Apparently he could teach her a few things, too.

"This...hardly seems...fair!" She seemed to be having trouble controlling her thoughts. "I want to—to touch—*Oh!*"

Chuckling, he slid her blouse off her arms, and helped her shrug out of her chemise. "Ye're telling me ye want me to remove my shirt as well?" he asked as he cupped her breasts, flicking his thumbs over her engorged nipples.

Her head was tipped back, her eyes closed. "Mmm. Shirt," she murmured, arching into his hand and making little movements with her pelvis he could only classify as desperate.

"Yer wish is my command, Treasure."

She made a little sound of disappointment when he dropped his hands away from her skin, but she soon grinned and began to help him, teasing him with her lips just as much as he'd done to her.

Their clothes seemed to fall off in a haze of cotton and desire, hands and fingers and lips everywhere. She ended up clambering off his lap in order to allow him to slide his trousers off, and he reached forward eagerly to help her with the clasp at her skirt's waist.

As the material fell around her legs, Cam's mouth went dry.

Or perhaps that was because of the wicked gleam in her eyes as she stepped out of the pile of her clothes and straddled his lap once more.

God Almighty, but she was already wet enough, he felt her slide along his thighs, her dew already seeping across his skin.

"Lass," he groaned, lowering his lips to her neck. "Ye're certain about this?"

And that's when her hand closed around his cock, and he jerked hard enough to slam his temple into her jaw.

She huffed softly, which might've been a giggle. "Oh, I'm certain. I've wanted this for... *Ai-ya*, Cam, this feels..."

She blew out a breath at the same time he sucked one in, and he felt as if they were sharing a life. "I promise ye, whatever *ye're* feeling, I'm feeling it ten times better." He shut his eyes, and with a groan, dropped his forehead to her shoulder. "Jade, ye're killing me."

"Shush. I'm exploring." And she was, her second hand joining her first, cupping, stroking, caressing. "Do you realize you're leaking?"

The sound which emerged from his throat was half laugh, half groan. "Ye're doing this on purpose, are ye no'? Torturing me."

"Well, you've seen all of me, and touched and tasted as well. I haven't had the opportunity." Humming, she dragged her palm all the way to the tip of his cock. "That night at the hotel, you moved your hand up and down your shaft like this. I watched in the mirror."

God Almighty, she *had*. It had made him so fooking aroused, to see her gaze on him masturbating to her own pleasure. And now…

Swallowing, he reached for himself, closing his hand around hers, trapping it against his skin. "Like this, lass," he managed hoarsely, guiding her gently in her strokes. "This is what feels good."

Her eyes were wide, staring down between them. "Why?"

"Because it's what I want to be doing to ye. Do ye understand?" She had the correct rhythm now, so Cam switched his hand to her curls, displayed delectably across his thighs. "I want to be *here*, moving that way."

She whimpered slightly as his fingers found her wet lips, spreading them farther, stroking them.

"It feels so good, Treasure, to be dipping in and out of ye." His fingers mimicked his words, as his thumb found her clitoris and his lips dropped to her shoulder. "I want to make ye *mine*."

Breathless, she managed, "But…*oh!* You said…Cam!"

"Easy, lass, take yer time."

The order did nothing to help, as she squirmed against his touch. Her fingers were still wrapped around his cock, but weren't moving. He assumed he'd distracted her.

She was rocking forward, gyrating her pelvis, as if trying to make him dip deeper, harder. He obliged, and she moaned.

"You want to be inside me?" she panted. "You're sure?"

He wanted it more than his next breath.

But all he could do was growl, "Aye," against her skin.

"Your heart—Oh!"

She would remember that, wouldn't she? He lifted her head and—fingers still inside her—met her eyes.

"I love ye, Treasure. My heart is verra much involved, and my cock kens it too."

Her lips curled upward, slowly at first, then growing into a brilliantly clear, genuine smile.

She leaned forward, her fingers caressing him. "Make love to me, Cam."

CHAPTER 10

HE SHOWED her how to shift forward, how to take her weight on her knees, how to *trust* him.

And then she sank down, encompassing him fully, settling against his lap until his cock was nestled *inside* her.

Where that dildo had once been.

Where she'd wanted him from the moment she'd set eyes on him.

Where he belonged.

With wide eyes, she pressed her naked chest against his, knees tight against his thighs, trying to come to terms with this feeling of *fullness*.

"Cam?" she whispered.

"Shh, lass. Dinnae move." His eyes were closed, his head tipped back against the chaise. "I'm trying not to die."

Well, that sounded promising. "Do you...like it?" she asked shyly.

"If I liked it anymore..." His lips twitched. "It feels fooking *amazing*."

Fooking amazing. She liked that.

And she would like it more if she could...

Despite his warning, she moved. Just a small, rocking motion, forward, then backward. It pushed her core against him, made her feel him more deeply.

And he groaned.

"Fooking amazing," she whispered.

She did it again, each movement causing pleasure to streak through her. Different kinds of pleasures, different kinds of streaks, each impossible to identify or name until she rocked again, duplicating the sensation. She was breathless, desperate.

In no time, she was drunk on the haze of pleasure, joy, ecstasy, which had settled over her.

She knew she was panting, knew she was using him, knew his big hands had settled on her hips and were helping her rock...but she could not seem to stop. Didn't *want* to stop.

Ai-ya, this was what she'd been needing!

"That's the way, lass," he murmured. "Ye feel it building, aye? Ye want to let it release?"

She whimpered in agreement, her eyes squeezed tight so she could concentrate on the sensations rocketing through her.

"Come for me—"

"No!" Her eyes flashed open as she remembered what happened the last time he'd commanded her. Already she could feel her release building, and tried to squeeze her legs together to control it.

"Nay?" His hands left her hips, stroking upward until he could cup her breasts. "Aye, lass, let me feel ye—"

"I want—I *need* you to spend as well, Cam!" she gasped. "That's the point of this exercise."

One corner of his lips twitched. "Exercise? I thought this was about yer pleasure."

"This is about *our* pleasure." She rocked against him again. "Please, Cam. I need this as much as I need..." Relaxing her thighs, she managed to sink down even farther, taking more of him inside her. "*This.*"

They both groaned.

He still didn't seem to understand. She took his cheeks in her hands, and captured his gaze. "I'm not a client, Cameron MacKay. I'm your bride. Make me *yours.*"

How could he deny such a order?

A long moment passed before he blinked, then snaked his arms around her back to pull her closer. "My bride," he repeated hoarsely. "My bride."

"Yes, Cam." Her hands fell to his shoulders, then around his neck, as their chests pressed flush against each other. "Yours."

With his hands on her buttocks, he showed her how to move, how to push herself up slightly, then sink down again, in the rhythm which made him groan. He seemed to like it slow and deep, the same as her, and *ai-ya*! It was empowering to feel his chest tightening, his breaths coming shorter and faster.

Knowing he was pushing toward the edge as surely as she was.

And then his fingers spread her arse cheeks, pulling—straining—urging, and one callused tip brushed against an area she'd never considered particularly erotic.

She was wrong.

Her climax burst over her, surprising her enough to let out a sort of shriek and tighten her hold on his neck as her inner muscles clamped around him.

She was strangling him.

And he froze. She thought she'd hurt him—not that she could do anything more than keen as her pleasure pushed her higher and higher—until he groaned soft and low, and she felt a surge of wet heat against her core.

There they sat, her choking the poor man, his face burrowed in her neck, their breathing ragged. She could *feel* him inside her. Not...not stretching, but just...he was *in* her. He was a part of her, now.

Now that she wasn't being distracted by wonderful, terrifying, delightful, all-consuming passion, she could focus on the way his pulse beat against the top of her opening. The way his breath cooled her skin. The way his sweat dampened his blond curls—the way they tasted when she gently brushed her lips across them.

The way she felt the smallest trickle of moisture where his face was pressed against her skin.

"Cam?" she murmured.

"I love ye," he whispered hoarsely. "I tried no' to, Treasure, because I kenned it wasnae what ye wanted, but..."

Gently, she loosened her hold on his neck, rocking back, allowing him to lift his head. They were still intimately attached, but now they could *see* each other.

And she saw she'd been right; he was blinking back moisture.

"I was wrong, Cam," she said with a soft smile, taking his cheeks between her palms once more. "I was wrong about you, and about marriage."

His blue eyes flicked back and forth between hers, searching for—for what? For the truth? This *was* the truth.

She leaned forward and captured his lips gently, showing him exactly what he meant to her. And she felt the moment he relaxed and accepted this. *Her.* Their future.

They kissed until she felt him hardening inside her once more. They kissed until their lips trailed across sweat-dampened skin, until they were both moaning and panting with need once more.

This time, he laid her down on the chaise, her feet planted on the floor, her legs spread wide. He knelt between her knees and kissed every inch of her. And when she was flying so high she thought she might touch the sun in her pleasure, he pushed into her once more.

Ai-ya, but *this* was joy! *This* was pleasure!

No wonder her mother had left her homeland to follow the man she loved.

Loved?

Yes, she loved Cam MacKay. Loved her husband.

That realization sent her crashing upward, her pleasure claiming her in a spiral of breathless delight.

And once more, he groaned low and thrust deep into her core, spending against her womb.

When he collapsed atop her, holding and stroking and murmuring, she felt...complete.

Also bone-weary, from the adventures of the day, and the fencing, and this marvelous new exercise. But mainly *complete*.

This was what she'd been missing. Not fooking, exactly, but companionship. Trust. Love. Someone to share her life with—the life she'd built. The life she hadn't missed so very much over these last days at The Cottage. Her managers were keeping Thacker Shipping in line, and now she didn't have to worry about Lord Buthert harming her business or her.

Because she had Cam. She loved Cam.

And she'd tell him that, as soon as she woke up.

———

SHE FELL ASLEEP UNDER HIM, and the realization made Cam smile. He stayed there until his cock—exhausted, the poor thing—slid out of her, and he was able to roll to one side. He gently cleaned her, expecting her to wake as he did...but he'd learned over the last few nights holding her that Jade was a sound sleeper.

It was just lucky she wasn't drooling now.

Once they were both cleaned up, he was tempted to just

curl up on the chaise and take her into his arms. But that was...

Well, frankly, it was a fooking terrible idea. He was too tall for the damn thing, and they'd likely both roll to their dooms. Or one would squish the other.

Chuckling at the image, he bent his knees to get his arms under Jade. He held his breath as he lifted, half-expecting her to shriek or wake up flailing. But instead she murmured softly in her sleep and pressed her cheek against his bare shoulder.

He had to smile. How could he not?

Whereas moments ago, he was soft and comfortable, lying atop her, now he felt...energized. The woman he loved trusted him—not just with her body, but with her safety. She was snuggled up against him, and he felt as if he could stand here forever, reveling in the feel of her trust.

But there was a big bed calling to him, and he turned his back on the waning fire and padded toward the rear of the house.

It was a bit of a struggle to pull the counterpane back and tuck her under it, while still holding her, but she did little more than murmur again and roll against the pillow, throwing one long leg out, as if trying to capture a sleeping partner.

By the time he finished, Cam was surprised to discover he wasn't at all tired. He'd been looking forward to crawling into bed beside her and taking her into his arms. Although he felt drained now, he was confident in a few hours he—and his cock—would be up for another master performance. The idea of taking her in his arms and waking her in the most erotic way...it was tempting.

And ye can still do it, ye dobber. Just give her a few hours' rest!

Aye, and he knew if he climbed in beside her, now, neither of them would get much rest. His blood was pounding, and frankly, he wouldn't mind something more to eat...

So he wrapped his kilt around himself and padded into the kitchen.

The last few days, they'd been reduced to cheese or eggs on bread, and whatever they could make from the increasingly sparse larder offerings. They *had* made another batch of cookies yesterday, and he gathered a few on his way to the closed-off parlor, to pour himself a brandy.

Standing there, barefoot and shirtless in the dark room, he realized he needed a way to occupy his mind. So he turned toward the cabinet where he'd stored the reports he hadn't found time to go over.

It was a bit of a juggle, getting the cookies, the brandy, and the reports back into the dining room, but once he deposited everything on the table, he was able to focus on building up the little fire once more.

When it was crackling merrily, he turned up the lamp to keep the outside darkness at bay, and began to fold and stack the clothing which had been thrown around the room in their earlier haste.

Was it any wonder he was smiling as he settled himself on the chaise? He'd likely never look at this room —this piece of furniture—the same way again. Without thinking of her sinking down atop him. Without remembering her claim she was *his*, his bride. Without remembering the way she tasted and felt and sounded and smelled and—

God Almighty, another *cockstand*?

Grinning wryly, he reached for the brandy. He didn't think he had enough energy left for another round. Best focus on sustenance and something boring.

Like last quarter's reports for Thacker Shipping.

His man of business had done a good job keeping Cam's involvement anonymous, and he'd become used to signing only his initials. After all these years, it was just simpler to keep his investment success a secret, he supposed. A quiet sort of victory which mattered only to him.

Jade kens ye're no' a whore, now.

Aye, that was true. Cam munched thoughtfully on a cookie as he stared at the fire. She *did* know he didn't keep the money his clients paid him, but she hadn't asked how he afforded the townhouse or scarlet leather fencing gloves or the thatching on The Cottage, or any of the other expenses associated with the extravagant lifestyle he led.

Those in Society who knew him as The Scot assumed he financed all this with his earnings, but he knew differently. And that had been enough, a sort of quiet nose-thumbing at those who thought themselves better.

So why had he kept his interest in Thacker Shipping a secret, especially from her? Originally, it had been because he didn't want anyone to realize he had the business acumen to manage an investment of this size. But once he realized who his latest client—who his new *bride*, thanks to his father's high-handedness!—really was, he should've told her.

But she'd come to him under the assumption he was courtesan. She hadn't realized the truth about him.

Now she does.

Aye, he needed to tell her, and apologize for not telling her sooner.

With a sigh, he flicked a few crumbs off the reports and tilted them so he could read them better. The company was doing brilliantly under Jade's management—not that he'd known it was being run by the *daughter* of "J. Thacker." Although Cam wasn't sure if that would have mattered to him.

But now that he knew her, he saw her hand in each of the decisions; the boldness, the commands, the daring new choices and destinations and cargo. She'd taken her father's kingdom and made it into an *empire*.

And in some way, Cam had helped.

The evening they'd sat in the parlor and she'd told him of her plans and goals, he hadn't expected her to be so *angry* about having to take on a silent partner. When he'd jumped at the opportunity, all those months ago, he'd assumed it was mutual.

But he'd learned she'd only done it because she needed to keep Buthert at bay, and planned to buy Cam out...and then the conversation had turned to the marriage by proxy, and he'd completely forgotten to bring up his silent partnership again.

But now he knew he'd helped her keep her company. Helped her to keep it running the way she wanted. And that was worth quite a lot to him.

A sound from the doorway had him turning, a cookie lifted halfway to his mouth.

It was Jade, looking adorably rumpled, her hair falling down around her shoulders, and the counterpane pulled snug about her.

From beneath the heavy fabric, he could see her bare ankles and feet peeking out. Knowing she was naked under that did nothing to help him in the cockstand department.

"Cam?" she asked with a yawn. "Come to bed."

He was grinning. "Aye, Treasure, I will. I was trying to give ye time to rest."

"I can't rest without you." She sounded grumpy as she padded across the floor, skirting the table and plopping beside him on the chaise. He got his reports out of her way in the nick of time, moving them to his lap as she snuggled up beside him.

With her cheek pillowed against his shoulder, it was easy enough to lift the half-eaten cookie to her mouth, and allow her to take a little nibble.

"Better?" he murmured.

She hummed. "The fire is nice."

He slid one arm around her, pulling her up closer. "I'm nice, too, eh? I planned on joining ye, I swear, I just thought ye could use the sleep."

"Before you climbed into bed with me?" He could hear the teasing in her voice. "No telling how long you'd last before I pulled you into my clutches."

Chuckling, he pressed a kiss to the crown of her head. "Insatiable."

"Only for you," she reminded him. "Now that I've finally convinced you to fook me, I'm making up for lost time."

Is that what she thought they were doing? Making up for lost time? Well, he'd fought it long enough, hadn't he? "Making love," he corrected softly, and liked the way her sigh sounded happy.

She took the cookie from his hand and popped it into her mouth. With her other hand, she reached across his lap and picked up the second page of the reports. "What's this?" she asked around the cookie.

And Cam considered stopping her. Considered pulling it from her hand, making an excuse, trying to explain things so it didn't look so bad.

But he knew it was time.

"It's my investments."

He felt the moment she realized what she was looking at; her shoulders stiffened and she slowly sat up. "This is my company," she whispered.

"Earlier, I told ye I didnae keep the money from the women I pleasured. Well…" He sighed, and tapped his finger against the edge of the paper she held. "I am verra good at choosing investments. I research and extrapolate, and I have a man of business I trust implicitly."

She didn't seem to be paying him attention. Instead, she shuffled through the papers and swallowed audibly. "These are the reports from last quarter. I went over them the week I met you."

"Aye. I'd already had an eye on the company, because of the profits it was posting. When the opportunity became available…" He shrugged.

Slowly, her wide eyes turned his way. "It's *you*? You're my silent partner? And you never told me?"

He tried for a charming grin. "That's the point of a silent partner, Jade. I didn't want anyone to ken."

"Not even *me?*" she hissed.

Well, shite. This wasn't going well. "To be fair, 'J. Thacker' is a common enough name—"

"I'm your *wife*, Cam!" The words exploded out of her as she scrambled to her feet, clutching the counterpane in one hand and the sheaf of papers in the other. "You *know* how hard it was for me to take a silent partner, how worried I've been!"

"I planned to tell ye." He kept his tone calm as he stood as well, his hands out, palms down in a conciliatory gesture. "As soon as ye mentioned that ye planned to buy out the partner, I meant to tell ye then. But we were talking about other things, and—"

She smacked him in the bare chest with the papers. "I cannot *believe* you just *forgot to mention it,* Cameron MacKay! You own shares of *my* company!"

"Our company," he corrected, and as soon as the words left his lips, he knew it was the wrong thing to say.

She shrieked in outrage, and this time threw the papers at him. They hit his chest and drifted to the floor, and he ignored them as he reached for her.

"Jade, be reasonable. I didnae ken who ye were—"

"And once you *did?* We've been stuck together for over a week—I can't believe I thought this *relaxing!* You knew my company name—"

He stepped forward, trying to gather her as she twisted away. "Treasure, I'm sorry—"

"Don't *Treasure* me, Cam!" She shrieked again, wordlessly, tossing her free hand up, then hurried to gather the blanket as she turned toward the door. "I'm so angry, I could scream."

"Ye *are* screaming," he pointed out unhelpfully.

"Arrgh!"

It was an impressive exit, he had to admit. She held herself like a queen, wrapped in her robes, stomping—actually stomping!—barefoot from the dining room. And he didn't think he'd ever actually *heard* someone say "aargh" out loud before, but there you go.

He followed her, arms still outstretched, and winced when she slammed the door to the bedroom. With her inside, and him most definitively *outside*.

The lock clicked into place.

With a sigh, Cam ran his hands through his hair and turned back to the dining room. No matter how uncomfortable that chaise was, it looked as if he'd be attempting to sleep on it tonight after all. Or perhaps that sofa in the damp parlor…

Ye idiot. Why did ye no' tell her sooner?

Because he'd been thinking with his cock when it came to Jade Thacker.

And now that he'd made her his in every sense of the word, he wasn't satisfied. No matter what Da said, no matter what the laws were concerning marriage by proxy, Jade was now *his*, and he'd fight to the death to keep her.

But she'd just made it clear she didn't want anything to do with him.

God Almighty, he was completely and utterly fooked, wasn't he?

CHAPTER 11

CAM DIDN'T GET to sleep until well after midnight, and then he slept fitfully. His stomach growled in hunger, and his heart ached. He felt stupid, for not finding a way to mention his involvement with Thacker Shipping earlier.

He didn't like feeling stupid, although it wasn't the first time.

Hell, the whole *point* of his investments was to remind himself he wasn't as stupid and useless as his family thought. He kept it a secret because he liked knowing something they didn't.

And now he'd kept it a secret from the one person he shouldn't.

Damnation.

So, aye, sleep was a long time coming, and not just because it ended up being easier to sleep on the carpet than the chaise.

His back ached and he had a stiff neck when he heard footsteps in the foyer. Grumpily, he rolled over to see dim light coming from the window, and knew it was after dawn. It must be Jade, up and about, although he didn't recognize her distinctive sharp footsteps.

The woman always strode about full of confidence, but not today.

The front door opened, then shut, and Cam felt as if The Cottage exhaled. She'd left.

She'd left?

Frowning now, he pushed himself to his feet, not sparing too much time to stretch the ache out of his neck. Knuckles kneading his lower back, he limped down the hall toward the bedroom. The door was ajar, and although it was *his* damn room, he still hesitated before nudging it open with his shoulder.

Little had changed since the day before, and yet…everything had. In a few short days, he'd become used to sharing a room with her. In a little over a week, he'd become used to *living* with her.

Loving her.

And now, after one argument, she'd left.

No' an argument, ye arse. She's angry because ye kept something important from her.

Och, that was true.

And her shoes are still here.

It took a moment to decipher why his subconscious thought her *shoes* were relevant, but once he did, he breathed a little sigh of relief.

Yesterday, the mud had made it difficult to wear shoes outside. Remembering that, she'd likely gone out for a little walk, perhaps for some fresh air, after being stuck inside for so long.

Or she's still livid, and doesnae want to be in the same building with ye.

Aye, or that.

But he was *trying* to remain positive, *thankyeverramuch.*

It was difficult.

Since she was out, he used the time wisely, changing into

trousers and a shirt and vest, washing and shaving and doing all those intimate tasks which were much easier to perform without the woman one loved staring at one. All while trying to remain positive.

This is certainly turning into a long just-getting-some-fresh-air stroll. She must be irate.

Maintaining positivity was becoming more difficult.

He slipped into the kitchen, and while the water boiled for tea, he prepared a simple breakfast of toast and jam—they'd made the bread together the day before yesterday—and apples fried in butter.

After, he plated the meal carefully, feeling surprisingly proud of how self-sufficient he'd become over the last week, and set the dining room table.

Still nae sign of her.

He took the time to sort through the reports he never did look through yesterday. And as he sipped his tea and munched on the sweet fruit, he perused the numbers. Aye, partnering with Thacker Shipping had been a wise financial choice.

Now, if only he could convince the owner he would make a sound partner.

He finished breaking his fast, and realized he could no longer avoid the gnawing worry in his stomach. She'd snuck barefoot from the house almost two hours ago; more than enough time for her to have walked off her irritation for him.

Or if not, at least enough time for her to be ready for some food.

Perhaps she's waiting for ye to come and fetch her?

Aye, that would be like his Treasure; determined to remain in control of the situation.

Well, he was no weakling, but he also had no trouble admitting when he was wrong. If she was waiting for him to grovel, he'd grovel.

Better go find yer groveling coat.

Where would she have gone? The cliffs weren't too dangerous, but if she didn't know the sea, the beach posed dangers. God forbid she'd gone back into those sea caves without him!

With each heartbeat, his worry increased. He tried to tell himself that she was the daughter of a sailor, and wouldn't be in any danger from a few waves, but it didn't work; each breath brought a tightening to his throat as he thought of her in danger.

Nay, she's just miffed at ye, and making ye squirm.

Aye, well, he'd squirm all she wanted, once he knew she was safe.

He was shoving his left arm into the sleeve of his groveling coat as he yanked open the front door. And that's when his eyes landed on the last person he expected.

"Son! I made it!" Argus MacKay's arms were wide, his dimples on display, his curls fading to a distinguished silver.

Scowling, Cam brushed past him, twisting his head back and forth as he searched for Jade.

"Cameron?"

"Hello, Da," he muttered distractedly, turning toward the cliffs. "Have ye seen Jade?"

His father's deep chuckle just made Cam's scowl deepen. "Ye've lost her already, eh? I leave the two of ye together for a day or two, and—"

"A day or two?" Cam wheeled on his father. "We've been stuck alone together for over a week, Da!" His arm swept to one side, encompassing the mud and the thatch in disarray and the distant roar of the sea. "Cut off from everyone because of the storm, and yer conniving."

Instead of appearing abashed—although Cam had never quite worked out what *bashed* meant in that context—his father hooked his thumbs through his braces and rocked back on his heels. "So she's well and truly compromised, eh? I kenned I could count on yer charm."

With a snarl, Cam threw himself toward his father, his fist already cocked—and managed to pull himself to a stop before he actually landed a blow.

The old man, damn him, just grinned knowingly.

Well and truly compromised.

Is that what his father had wanted? Cam had fought it—oh, how he'd fought—but aye, Jade was his now.

"She's my *bride*," he snarled instead, "is she no'?"

Da's grin just grew wider. "I think ye should invite me in for a bit. Perhaps some coffee and something sweet, and ye can explain how ye managed to lose her already."

Cam's head swung back around, peering toward the surf. "I didnae lose her. We…quarreled. She went out for a walk, and hasnae returned."

Chuckling, his father slapped him on the back. "She just needs a bit to cool down, laddie. Our Jade is a powerful young woman, but can be hot-tempered at times."

Our Jade? "No' that I've noticed," Cam mumbled.

"That's because ye've done such an excellent job charming the lass." The way the older man winked as he nudged his son left no doubt to what sort of *charm* he meant.

But Cam wasn't convinced. "She's been gone a while, Da. I'm worried."

His father followed the direction of his gaze, and snorted derisively. "John Thacker's daughter would *no'* be so rude as to drown in the Firth, laddie, ye have my word. Now, coffee." When Cam turned a glare on him, Da merely winked. "And cookies, if ye have any. My coach can wait."

As he waved good-naturedly to his coachman, Cam relented. "Nae coffee. We're on deprivation rations, remember?" He sighed in acceptance as he turned toward the door. "I made tea."

His father preceded him, stomping his boots off beside the umbrellas. "Looks a bit different, lad," he near-bellowed. "I still think ye need a houseful of servants."

"I could've used them this past week," Cam muttered, leading the way into the dining room, thinking that Mrs. Higgins on the premises would've made his life easier. And he likely could've managed to keep his cock under his kilt with a maid or three flitting about. "The place hasnae weathered the storm as gracefully as I would like."

His father laughed and sat down at the place Cam had set for Jade. "This bread's a bit auld. Ye're going to fix it up now that ye will be married, I assume? Furnish a few more rooms—the bairns will need a nursery—and move in some staff?"

Bairns.

Cam swallowed, his knees suddenly going weak enough to necessitate a grab for the back of the nearest chair. Bairns with Jade. He had no idea how she thought of the idea, but after what they'd shared last night—*twice*—she could very well be carrying his son or daughter right now.

A little gray-eyed imp with her mother's determination and her father's charm.

God Almighty, the thought was terrifying and wonderful all at once.

Da hummed in appreciation. "These apples are delightful. Have yer cook send the recipe up to the Highlands, eh?"

"I made them," Cam mumbled.

"What's that?"

Cam took a deep breath, and straightened. "I made them, Da. And Jade and I made the bread. I told ye, we've been surviving on our own, thanks to the storm."

His father was gaping at him. "And ye've...learned to bake."

Oh, for fook's sake, it wasn't like he'd learned brain

surgery! "We had a recipe book, Da," he managed dryly. "I'm no' completely useless."

The older man still stared, his fork frozen halfway to his lips. Finally, he shook his head and took the bite. "I never thought ye useless, son," he muttered around the apples.

But he *did*, didn't he? That was why Cam had hid who he really was for so long; a sort of perverse fulfillment that he *wasn't* as useless as his family thought. "I have plenty of talents, Da."

"Aye, and the ladies pay dearly for them," his father said with a wink.

Cam rolled his eyes, knowing he shouldn't have bothered with this conversation. "I meant *investments.* I'm good at managing money."

"Well then, ye and yer future wife will have plenty to talk about, eh?"

Future wife. And before, Da had said *Ye will be married.*

Cam's knuckles tightened around the back of the chair.

"Da...what's this bullshite about marriage by proxy?"

His father's attention jerked up from his tea. "Bullshite, as ye say." He was grinning. "It got ye both here, did it no'?"

They weren't married. Over the pounding of the pulse in his ears, Cam heard himself ask, "Was that yer plan? To get us both here, in the hopes I'd—" His voice faltered, and he swallowed. "*Compromise* her?"

"It worked, did it no'?" His father's chuckle was good-natured. Charming. Annoying as *fook*. "I meant to arrive sooner, of course, but everything from here to Inverness is blasted mud!"

They weren't married.

Jade wasn't his wife.

But she's still yers.

Cursing, Cam whirled for the door, determined to find

her. If he wasn't married to her, and she was still angry with him...

He had to find her.

"Jade!" he called as soon as he stepped out of The Cottage. *"Jade!"* He cupped his hands around his mouth and took three long strides for the cliffs. *"Jaaaade!"*

"Ye think this is more than just a walk to blow off steam, laddie?" His father was standing in the portico, carrying his teacup in one hand. "Why are ye so frantic?"

"Because I need to ken she's alright," Cam snapped without turning. "I'm going to check the beach."

From behind him, his father called, "I'll check up here."

But a half hour later, Cam had to admit the truth: she wasn't anywhere around The Cottage. He could hire an experienced tracker to confirm, but to his untrained eye, it seemed as if a set of bare footprints fought through the mud toward the lane leading toward the village.

"*Fook!*" he hissed, slamming his toe into the stone of the portico. "*Shite fook shite!*"

"Calm down, son." Da looked uncharacteristically somber as he folded his arms across his chest. "We'll find her."

"What if we dinnae?" Cam scrubbed a hand over his face. "What if she's gone into the village? What if she's on a train back to London?"

"Well..." The older man shrugged pragmatically. "We'll find her in London, then. Besides, ye said she didnae pack her belongings."

The reminder did much to calm Cam's frantic helplessness. "That is..." He frowned toward the distant village. "That is correct. And she wouldnae have boarded the train in bare feet."

His father nodded as he waved his arm for his coachman to join them. "Is it possible she just went into the village?"

Cam shook his head thoughtfully. "I cannae imagine she'd go *there* barefoot either," he murmured.

His father's coachman had climbed down from the ornate carriage and was picking his way carefully through the mud. When he approached, Da summarized the situation in curt tones.

"Ye'll bring my son to the village, while I wait here in case my niece returns."

The young man was nodding agreeably. "Aye, milord." He turned to Cam. "And if I might suggest, once we reach the village, ye consider asking the other lord for help? He's likely honor-bound to offer assistance if a lady is missing."

Cam was frowning, as his father barked, "What other lord?"

The coachman glanced between the two of them. "I dinnae ken his name, but we passed his coach this morning, right afore we reached The Cottage. He was barreling back toward the village as if the verra hounds of hell were on his heels!"

What in the name of Satan and his little minions would a lord be doing out *here*? Cam stepped toward the servant. "Ye're certain it was a lord's carriage?"

"Aye, it had to be. Black, and covered in so much gilt, it was hard to believe the thing hadn't collapsed under the weight."

A terrible suspicion slammed into Cam, and he felt his blood freezing as he asked, "Can ye remember anything else about it?"

"Och, aye! The horseflesh weren't matched, which made me think mayhap they was rented. These lords always travel in style, ye ken. The bloke on the seat gave me a right polite nod, though, so I did the same in return." The coachman pursed his lips as he considered. "Och, and the crest! A giant *'B'* it was, surrounded by gold curlicues and swoops, what are they called?"

But Cam didn't answer. He'd turned horrified eyes to his father, who was looking just as shocked as he was.

It was possible there were multiple dandies in Britain who went about in jet-black, highly gilded coaches. But there was only one whose family crest was an ornate *B*.

And he had an inheritance's worth of reasons to snatch a barefoot Jade from the lane, and rush her toward the village.

"*Buthert.*"

CHAPTER 12

HE DIDN'T TIE her hands, which was convenient. Jade's thighs ached after the vigor of last night, and she found herself walking gingerly; it was nice not to also have to worry about keeping her balance while bound.

Of course, Lord Buthert hadn't been exactly considerate of her comfort, oh no. Likely he just didn't want to attract the undue attention which parading her bound through the streets would've warranted. As it was, her bare feet were gaining more than a few stares.

Jade did rather regret leaving her shoes in the room this morning when she decided to slip outside for a bit of fresh air. But how was she supposed to know that as soon as she stopped at the gate, her head tipped back to enjoy a bit of the long-awaited sunshine, a black coach would come barreling out of nowhere and screech to a stop beside her, tossing mud all over her blue skirts?

And how in the world could she have guessed who was *inside* said coach, holding a small pistol and demanding she join him?

Ai-ya, what else could she do except climb in with him?

Briefly, she'd considered removing some article of clothing and dropping it into the muck beside the lane, so Cam—upon waking and discovering her missing—would know what had happened to her.

Her shoe would've been her first choice, had she actually been wearing them. Otherwise, she was limited. Dropping her skirt on the ground made little sense, and she'd been certain Buthert wouldn't allow her the time to unbutton her blouse. She was reaching for the pins holding her bun in place—hoping Cam would be able to see them amid the mud—when Buthert had growled something nasty and shoved the barrel of the pistol into her ear.

All things considered, it had made more sense to do as he said.

She had assumed she knew Lord Buthert, but the ride to the village had been an eye-opening experience. The man was...miffed.

"A week! A bloody *week!*" he ranted, waving the pistol about in the dim interior of his carriage as it trundled toward the village. "I have been stuck in this *hellhole*, this country *nowhere*, full of Scots and diseased livestock and *chickens*, for a full bloody week!"

"Diseased livestock, milord?" she murmured, knowing she shouldn't antagonize him, but unable to stop the clarification.

"There are *animals* in the middle of the *village*, wandering around, making *sounds!*"

Oh dear. He was speaking in italics now. Forget *miffed*, Buthert was *irate*. "What sorts of sounds, milord?"

The man—whom so many called handsome, with his thick, dark mustache—scowled as he gestured with the pistol. "You know. *Moo. Cluck.*"

"Oink?" she offered, leaning out of the way of the barrel of the gun. She thought it was one of those small, cleverly made American derringers.

"Do not be silly, girl," he barked. "I have learned, to my chagrin over the last week, that pigs do not say *oink*. Rather, it is a sort of enraged *mmmmrrrraaarrrrrooor.*"

Jade's brows rose, impressed despite herself at his impression. Under what circumstance would Buthert have heard an enraged pig?

"So you are saying, milord, these normal animals, who were roaming the village, were making normal animal sounds? Were any of them actually diseased?"

"Some of them must have been. They sounded diseased."

Since he was holding the gun, Jade thought it prudent to nod and murmur, "Good point, milord."

"And the people were no better! They are *Scots!*"

Jade pressed her lips together.

"And *diseased* Scots, I am certain! Do you know where I have spent the last week?"

She told herself this was Cam's home, not hers. It wasn't her place to become irritated by the man's insults, but she did, all the same. "I assume in the village," she managed, hiding her pique.

"In the village!" He was back to waving the gun around. "In their laughable excuse for a hotel!"

I believe there's a set of rooms over the pub, but they're often in use by one of the local whores.

It was easy to remember Cam's words. *All* of Cam's words —including the part about loving her—but Jade pushed those memories aside, knowing she couldn't afford to be distracted. She kept her mouth shut, not wanting to encourage Buthert's anger, but he continued his rant anyhow.

"It is not even a hotel, really! And can you believe they wanted to begrudge me a room when I arrived? Pouring down rain, and they did not think my money was good enough for their squalor!"

Unable to keep quiet any longer, Jade tried to quell her

frosty tone when she said, "I believe the rooms are mostly spoken for, are they not? By businesswomen."

"*Whores!* How do you think I managed to procure a room? Buy buying their attention as well!" Muttering in anger, he slumped back against the squabs, and Jade eyed the gun. But before she could make a move, he waved his arm again. "A week trapped inside because of the bloody horrible weather, sleeping on a lice-ridden bed, fucking a lice-ridden whore!"

Unabashedly, the dark-haired man scratched at his crotch, and Jade turned her attention to the window, wondering if, were she about to vomit, she could manage to aim for his lap.

"Oh, did I hurt your delicate sensibilities, Miss Thacker?" he sneered. "Are you surprised to learn I have a temper, and am through trying so politely to woo you?"

"Not really, no," she murmured quietly, not sure if she wanted him to hear her or not.

"Yes, that's right, my little half-breed," he sneered, the pistol once more rising toward her forehead. "*You're* the reason I'm stuck in this diseased little piece of hell, bored to death with the same fish stew, the same watered ale, and the same whore's mouth! *You!*"

Yes, she'd rather been afraid of that.

"If you had just accepted my generous marriage proposal, I would not have had to follow you all the way to the middle of Nowhere, Scotland. Do you know they're *proud* of their little village? The place is disgustingly quaint—just another word for backward—and I would have never set foot here if I had not learned you'd purchased a ticket here, and followed you!"

Taking a deep breath, she turned back to the man who'd once declared his undying love for her. Of course, since he'd also—during the course of their acquaintance—declared his undying love for Beake's Mustache Wax, pickled beets, and Disraeli's foreign policies, she hadn't given it much credence.

"Shall I apologize, milord?" She hoped she sounded far calmer than she actually felt.

"It would be an excellent start to our marriage!" He leaned forward suddenly, the barrel of the gun unerringly pointing between her eyes. "But do not think I will refrain from showing you my displeasure! Those whores only whetted my appetite, although I have been told you have spent these last days sheltering with Cameron MacKay. That useless sack of piss must have *surely* deflowered you by now, but I find myself in a generous mood. You will say nothing of this adventure, and Society will still accept you as Lady Buthert, as I have planned."

Ai-ya. There was certainly plenty to sift through in that speech.

Jade had bristled at the insult to Cam, and had to refrain from announcing she was in love with the man. There'd also been a brief flicker of fear—greater fear—at the mention of his displeasure. And then, of course, there'd been the marriage reference.

She opted to address that first. "You still expect to be married to me, milord?"

There, that sounded much more polite than, *You complete nutter, why would I marry you?*

Unfortunately, the gun didn't waver. "It is not what I *expect*, you little slut, but what I will be *achieving*. In three weeks, the rest of your inheritance will come to you. Or, if you are married, to your husband."

Jade swallowed a completely stupid lump of emotion which had somehow lodged its way in her throat. She *knew* Buthert was only after *Gung Gung's* money, but to hear it stated so blandly was maddening.

She twined her fingers together in her lap and focused her gaze on them, trying to seem harmless. In a small voice, she said, "And you need the money for your estate."

"Of course! *All* lords need money for their estates! That is why marriages exist between men like me, and the daughters of the middle class! Why else would I be so desperate to marry someone with such obviously inferior blood?"

Jade was eighty percent certain he was referring to her mother, but opted not to push the issue. However, hearing his plan to marry her made her feel better about the gun in her face.

"Since you plan to marry me to gain my inheritance, perhaps you might lower your weapon?" She tried for a soft smile. "You need me alive."

"And willing," he snarled, although he did lower the pistol. "Keep in mind, you *will* claim to be marrying me of your own free will, or I will shoot you."

"And kill the only opportunity of gaining my grandfather's money?"

He scoffed. "I'll aim for something useless, like your leg. You can still sign cheques with one leg, right?"

She was about to explain to him that no, she'd be in far too much pain and also busy interviewing lawyers to prosecute him, to bother signing over her money. But the coach had stopped, and at that moment, Buthert's servant pulled the door open with a blank expression. "We have arrived, milord."

"Excellent!" Buthert beamed, then gestured for Jade to precede him from the vehicle. "You first, and remember, I do not mind a lame wife." As she began to move, his gaze turned thoughtful. "Or perhaps infection will set in, and you will survive only a few days past your twenty-fifth birthday, upon which time you will be buried by your grieving and suddenly quite a bit wealthier husband."

It might have been terrifying, to hear his plan spoken so boldly. But instead, Jade had to swallow down laughter. Slightly maniacal and demented laughter, certainly, but laughter at his plan, because it was impossible.

She couldn't marry Buthert, because she was already married to Cam MacKay.

And yes, last night had been...

Well, it had frankly been a riot of emotions, hadn't it?

First there'd been the way he opened up to her, told her so much. He'd been hiding so much of himself—who he *really* was—from everyone. Everyone but her. She'd been so bleeding *happy* he'd trusted her enough to share the truth about his life with her.

And then, of course, the sex had been spectacular. Beyond spectacular, but there was no need to belabor the point, really.

And then after previously indicated spectacular sex, she'd learned...he *hadn't* told her everything. Oh, he'd apologized, but she'd just been so angry—at him, and at herself for being angry—she'd punished them both by locking him out of the bedroom.

Which, about thirteen minutes later, she was able to admit was a stupid and cruel decision. But she was stubborn and proud, and so she went to sleep cold and lonely.

But not before having a *really good* cry, and deciding she was being unreasonable. Cam had apologized about keeping his involvement a secret, and if she were being honest with herself, there hadn't really been all that much time between the confessing-all and the spectacular sex, so she shouldn't be too miffed he hadn't got around to telling her everything.

By this morning, she'd been ready to apologize to him for her reaction...but when she crept into the dining room to see him stretched out on the floor so pitifully, well, she felt guilty all over again. Perhaps it was cowardice which convinced her she so desperately needed a calming walk in the fresh air to soothe her spirits.

Either way, had Cam awakened, she would've told him she loved him, and while she was still shocked at the strange way their lives had become intertwined before they even knew each other's names, she wasn't sorry for it.

No, in fact, quite the opposite. If she was going to take on a partner for her business, she could think of no one she'd rather have than the man she'd chosen for her partner in life: her husband, the man she loved.

The man who'd better get around to figuring out where she was, so he could come facilitate the rescue, before she had to explain to Buthert why she couldn't marry him.

That's when she felt the barrel of the pistol dig into her back, which returned her to the present, and the fact she was strolling along—barefoot!—through the local village, garnering all sorts of stares as they dodged perfectly healthy pigs and chickens, on their way toward…

A blacksmith's shop.

A legitimate blacksmith's shop.

As if the last fifty years of technological advancements hadn't been made, and metal was still shaped by burly shirtless men in leather aprons pounding with hammers. *Barbaric.*

Actually, there was a sign over the admittedly quaint door: **Ye Olde Fashioned Blacksmith Shoppe (inquire within about tours and souvenirs).**

Hmm.

Buthert snapped, "Hurry! I heard the man takes a lunch break!" as he nudged her toward the blacksmith shop.

Why in the world would he be bringing her to a blacksmith *now*? It was impossible to deny he was marching her toward the door, but *why*? She couldn't even imagine him commissioning a ring from such a place, not when London was full of jewelers who could likely produce any number of engagement rings on short notice.

"Smith!" he called as soon as he followed her into the darkened shop. "Smith, we have need of you!"

As Jade's eyes adjusted to the dim lighting, she was surprised by what she saw.

This really *was* an "old fashioned blacksmith shop", in the same way The Cottage was *actually* a cottage.

There was a wide, open floor of pounded dirt and scattered hay, and the place was lit, not by lanterns or lamps, but genuine torches. Like, dipped-in-tar, stinking-up-the-place, staining-the-roof-joists *torches*.

There were weapons lining the walls; swords and maces and even a few shields hanging on display. Along the back wall was a cold forge and anvil, roped off with heavy string, as if to keep back curious onlookers, if a blacksmith *did* decide to perform a demonstration or something.

"Smith!" bellowed Buthert again.

And this time, he was answered by a call from behind the little door which led from the rear of the building. "Coming, coming!" When the man stepped through, Jade caught a peek of the room behind—it looked like a home—but was rather more distracted by the man himself.

This was *not* a blacksmith.

For one thing, he looked younger than her. He was dressed neatly in a brown suit, and his hair was smoothed back— likely with the same pomade Buthert loved so dearly. One of his spindly arms rose to push his spectacles back up the bridge of his nose, then tapped against the clipboard he carried.

"I'm terribly sorry, sir, madam," he said with a faint brogue, "but today's tour has been cancelled."

Due to lack of interest, Jade would have to say.

"Fool!" snapped Buthert, jabbing her again with the pistol and forcing her forward a few steps. "We're not here for the tour! We're here to be married!"

It was difficult to say who was more surprised.

The young caretaker's eyes widened so much, his spectacles were in danger of falling off again. Jade herself stepped forward—out of gun-poking distance—and turned to Buthert.

"Married?" she repeated, just as the young man blurted, "Ye cannae be married here!"

But Buthert scowled, hurrying to hide the small pistol between his palm and thigh, as if hoping to perpetrate the falsehood she was here willingly. "Of course we can be married here!" He gestured with his other hand toward the forge. "That is an anvil, is it not? You are a blacksmith? I know this is not Gretna Green, but you can marry us. Quickly, now!"

The young man must not have noticed the gun after all, because he was shaking his head, a superior, intellectual smile settled across his face. "Sir—"

"*My lord*," snapped Buthert, clearly at the end of his patience.

"*Milord*," began the caretaker again. "I am no' a blacksmith. My grandfather was the last full-time smith in the area, and my father performs some farrier work as needed—"

"Then get *him* in here to marry us!"

Despite his quickly unraveling temper, Jade cleared her throat, trying to turn the man's attention to her. "Lord Buthert, do you mean to say you've brought me *here* to be married. Now? Today?"

The dark-haired, spoiled lordling snarled and stepped forward, his arm jerking as if he wanted to raise the gun, but remembered at the last moment why he could not. "You will not defy me, Jade! I told you what would happen!"

"Oh, yes," she managed with a completely bland tone, glancing toward their witness. "Any woman would be thrilled to become Lady Buthert. But this isn't a church."

The caretaker raised a finger unhelpfully. "It's a smithy."

"I can tell it's a smithy, you dolt!" Buthert wheeled on the other man. "And this is Scotland! Anyone who reads knows that fast marriages can be performed in Scotland! Over an anvil in Gretna Green! There is an entire genre of literature predicated on this fact!"

Face beginning to go purple, Buthert was stalking toward the young caretaker, who was retreating. Jade used that opportunity to sidle closer to the wall, where the displayed weapons really weren't all that well secured.

She didn't have time to be picky, so she carefully—without turning fully away from her captor—managed to remove what looked like a two-handed saber.

A *claidheamh.*

Ai-ya, had it only been yesterday she'd teased Cam about his training? She'd never held such a weapon, of course, but as she tucked it behind her back, hoping her skirts would shield it, she decided the heft was similar to the sabers her father's man had sparred with.

Across the room, the poor young man looked ready to bolt, as he stammered out an explanation for why all of Buthert's plans were absolute rubbish.

Feeling rather more certain of herself now she had a blade in hand, Jade found herself grinning as she called out to him, "Milord, a question, please?"

Her captor whirled about. When he saw her grin, he took two steps toward her.

"Buthert," she began, still smiling. "Am I correct in assuming this entire asinine misadventure—your presence in this village, your abduction of me—is grounded in the belief that Lord Brougham's Act of 1856...just never occurred?"

He turned toward her, brows drawn in like a confused hedgehog, and she continued. "Since its passing, Scotland requires two people who are attempting to be married here also *live* here. I don't remember how long."

"Three weeks," squeaked the young caretaker.

Jade nodded, her eyes on Buthert. "It's been years since you could just abduct an heiress and take her over the border and bribe a blacksmith to wed the pair of you."

Buthert was sputtering, but she couldn't tell if it was because of her lack of deference, her announcement in front of a witness that she was being abducted, or the realization his scheme was failing.

In order to help him decide which reason to be angry about, she added a, "You idiot," for good measure.

That worked. His dark eyes hardened, then narrowed, as he stalked toward her. "Lord Bingbang's Marriage Act, bitch? I pay no attention to such nonsense."

"No, clearly," she agreed dryly, edging out of his way while keeping the sword hidden. "You're not a woman with a fortune to protect from unscrupulous men, like you."

His breath hissed. *"Unscrupulous?"*

"Oh, pardon me." She turned fully to face him, now that she stood in the center of the open space, and pulled the sword from behind her. "I should have called you a sack of diseased cow shite. I believe that's the local colloquialism."

She was mad. Or deliriously happy. That was the only explanation for why she felt like laughing now, remembering Cam's description of the spoiled, disgusting lordling. Feeling full of power, she settled into a guard position.

But Buthert, to give him his due, was supremely unimpressed by her sword. "You think to threaten me, bitch?" he scoffed. "I am a member of the London Fencing Club! I have faced off against the best."

"But you didn't beat them, did you?" She had no way of knowing that, but judging from the way his face purpled once more, her mocking had been aimed true.

He whirled toward the wall and ripped down the first blade he could reach, a wicked rapier design which had been popular two hundred years ago. He settled easily into *en guard*, and Jade began to regret choosing a heavier sword.

From the corner of her eye, she saw the caretaker scurry away, and breathed a little sigh of relief. Hopefully he was running to get help. At least she didn't have to worry about hurting him.

Because she had plenty of other things to worry about already.

With a wild yell—possibly intended to intimidate his opponent, although it made him sound like a constipated walrus—Buthert attacked. His swing was clearly a feint, and Jade parried easily, giving ground in order to test his skill.

He was good, but not as good as her. Unfortunately, he had chosen a weapon he was actually familiar with, and was stronger than she was. After a few moments of steel clashing against steel, it became apparent she wouldn't be able to last very long against him.

He's not nearly as much fun to spar with as Cam.

Cam! She only had to get out of this mess, and she vowed she'd *run* back to The Cottage to tell him how much she loved him. How much she wanted to spend the rest of her life sparring with him, sharing with him. And of course, making love to him.

"I cannot tell where you trained, bitch," Buthert was panting, "but you have passable skill for a woman."

She pressed her lips together, determined not to waste her breath on answering his mocking, and concentrated on a backhanded swing. He only just managed to block it, but she'd anticipated that.

Instead of retreating, she dropped the point of her blade downward, sweeping across the back of his left hand, which still held the gun.

Not for long, though. With a startled squawk, Buthert dropped the pistol into the dirt, already stepping back, which allowed her to dart forward.

The pistol was heavier than it looked, and hurt like the

blazes when she kicked it out of the way. Her hiss of pain accompanied her sudden shift to her other foot to accommodate the pain in her bare foot.

Taking advantage of her distraction, Buthert shook the blood from his hand and advanced.

Without a choice, Jade limped backward, the *claidheamh* held low, prepared to meet his attack. But she didn't have to.

Because she backed right into a solid wall of chest. A chest she recognized even without turning around.

Cam.

"Picking on lasses now, Buthert?" her love drawled. "I wish I could say I was surprised."

That's when a blade rose beside her, and she realized Cam had either come prepared, or he'd pilfered from the ancient smithy as well. She found her shoulders relaxing, her guard dropping.

He was here. He would take care of this.

For once, she was happy not to have to be in control. Happy to let him take command, happy to have *him* tell her what to do.

Not the only time.

Ai-ya, of course there was the making love. *Come for me, Treasure.* How could she deny *that* order?

"Are ye well, love?" he murmured, as she pressed back against him.

"Aye." She took a deep breath, and felt her tension ease as she released it. "Now I am."

But Buthert sneered. "What a touching reunion. But you must know I will not allow Lord Binglebam's Act of 1865—"

"Fifty-six," she corrected.

"—to ruin my plans!" he snarled, as if she hadn't interrupted. "You *will* be my wife, Jade Thacker, and your inheritance *will* be mine. And your father's shipping company will be mine as well."

"First of all…" She placed the tip of her blade in the dirt, which she knew was a major *faux pas,* but was feeling cocky. "It is *my* company, not my father's. Second, you cannot possibly own all of it, ever, because my silent partner owns a large share, and I trust him implicitly." Behind her, she heard Cam's breath catch. "And finally…"

With a big smile, she stepped out of the way, so Cam could face Buthert directly. "Finally, milord, I am married already. To Cam MacKay, the finest man I know."

"Married?" Buthert sputtered.

Her grin grew. "By proxy."

"How is *that* legal, when the anvil and the blacksmith and all that is not?" The dark-haired lord was turning almost apoplectic.

Was it her imagination, or did she see Cam wince as he shifted into a guard position? She didn't have a chance to consider, because at that moment, Buthert released another yodel, and attacked.

Her eyes followed Cam's swift parry, then *his* lunge, and she realized she was holding her breath. This wasn't for points, wasn't for sport. This was a bloody battle, and it frightened her more now that Cam was involved, than when it had been her facing Buthert's blade.

"It's no', ye ken."

The announcement, spoken in a low voice from behind her, had Jade's attention jerking about to see Cam's father, looking chagrined and not at all concerned for his son.

"Uncle Argus!" She threw her arms around her aunt's husband, while keeping her attention on Cam's battle. "What isn't?"

"Marriage by proxy, with neither party present, and neither one consenting."

She stole a glance at him. "What?"

"It's no' legal, lass. I'm sorry for lying to ye both, to get ye to The Cottage."

At that moment, Buthert lunged, and Jade's heart jolted as she realized what that meant. "We're not married?" she whispered as Cam's steel clanged.

The sound dragged her attention back to the fight, eyes wide and heart in her throat, to see Cam thrust forward, his weight on his front leg in a risky move, and slam his sword *hard* against his opponent's blade.

Buthert dropped his rapier.

Before she could blink, Cam was in front of him, the edge of his blade resting against the spoiled lordling's throat, both of them breathing heavily.

She stepped toward them, unsure what she could do, but knowing she couldn't allow Cam to ruin his future. His future with her. Whether or not they were married.

But it was Buthert who stopped her.

"You think you could kill me?" he sniffed haughtily. "A half-breed Scottish layabout whore?" His eyes flicked to Jade. "You two deserve one another."

"Thank ye," growled Cam, but Jade was already moving again.

"Yes, thank you, milord," she declared, flattening her palm against Cam's lower back in a show of support she hoped he understood. "Because we have found one another, and there's nothing you can do about it. You've lost."

Buthert's chin rose imperiously, obviously trying to detract from the fear in his eyes as the blade at his neck never wavered. "Do not be ridiculous. I cannot *lose*, not to the likes of *him*. I'm a lord, and you cannot hurt me."

"Nay," growled Cam. "I cannae *kill* ye. But I wouldnae want that stain on my soul, anyhow. But I *can* hurt ye."

"Wha— " Before Buthert could stammer out the question, Cam's fist cocked back and he let fly.

Thank goodness he moved his sword away from the other man's neck, or there might've been accidental bloodshed after all.

As it was, Buthert went sailing backward, slamming into the wall of the ancient smithy hard enough to rattle the weapons hanging there. Blood streaming from his nose, he sank to the floor.

And to Jade's surprise, Uncle Argus marched up to him and toed him in the side. "I'm a lord too, laddie, and I'm allowed to hurt ye all I want, because I can meet ye in court. Dinnae forget that."

Then he turned and plopped himself down *atop* the supine man, his elbows resting on his knees as he grinned up at Cam and Jade. "He's still out cold, but it was a fine speech, eh?"

"Aye, Da." Cam's voice sounded hoarse.

Uncle Argus made little shooing motions. "I'll keep an eye —and an arse—on this puddle of piss. The pair of ye have some things to say to one another, I think."

Jade didn't need any more encouragement.

She immediately threw her arms around Cam. "I'm so sorry."

"Nay." His voice was hoarse, his body stiff, as he pulled her against him. "It is I who should be sorry. Treasure, I should've told ye sooner—"

"Hush," she commanded, pushing herself upward to brush her lips across his. "I trust you. I should've trusted that you would have told me, I just hadn't given you enough time."

His expression softened. "That...is true. So ye forgive me?"

"Aye," she drawled in imitation of him. "But only if you kiss me again."

He did, but the kiss was...well, frankly, thoroughly unsatisfying.

"What was that?" she muttered as he pulled away, and she unconsciously followed him.

"*That*, my insatiable bride, was to whet yer appetite."

Blinking, she frowned up at him. "I'm already hungry." She pushed her hips forward so he'd understood what she meant.

"Fine." He blew out a breath as he rolled his eyes. "Then it was to remind ye that my father is *right over there*, watching us."

"Keep it up, laddie!" Uncle Argus called from across the room. "Ye've almost got her convinced!"

"He can't hear us," she assured Cam with a grin, "but he can see us!"

Cam pretended to frown, but she could see the sparkle in his eyes. "So please try to refrain from kissing me."

"I shall *try*," she promised with a dramatic sigh. "Besides, there's something important we must discuss."

"Aye, Treasure. My father told me—"

"I love you, Cameron MacKay."

Well, *that* shut him right up. His jaw dropped, his mouth actually open enough she could see his tongue trying to form words, and his blue eyes…

The look in his beautiful eyes slowly turned from shocked and disbelieving to awe-struck.

His mouth closed, his throat worked as he swallowed. Finally, he whispered, "Ye do?"

Made suddenly shy by his response, Jade felt her cheeks warm, but she held his gaze. "I'm so sorry I took so long to tell you, Cam. You are a special man. A brilliant, caring man, who deserves all the love in the world. And the fact you're *surprised* by this makes me love you even more."

"Nae one has ever—" He shook his head. "Ye're certain?"

"Of course." Her lips softened into a smile. "Cam, I love you, and I am honored and humbled you feel the same way about me. I look forward to spending the rest of my life with you."

He was staring down at her, and she could see his mind

working frantically behind his gaze. Slowly, his lips began to curl. "Ye ken what I think?"

"What's that?" she whispered.

"I think I ought to kiss ye after all."

She was already pushing herself up on her toes. "Uncle Argus will understand."

This kiss was long and deep and tender, and eventually interrupted by Cam's father whooping in excitement from across the room.

"Did she say aye, laddie?" he bellowed. "Get her to say aye for real this time!"

Cam rolled his eyes, but his arms tightened around her.

"Treasure, ye've already given me a true gift. But..." Surprisingly, he seemed ill-at-ease, and glanced at his father. "I received some bad news with Da's arrival. He admitted he— Well, I'm no' quite sure how to tell ye..."

Jade smiled, knowing exactly what he was trying to confess. "I think, all things considered, we'd better go visit a vicar. A *real* one, who can *really* marry us."

Cam's expression cleared. "So ye ken the truth?"

"Aye, yer father confessed while ye were in the midst of yer daring-do."

His lips twitched, and he squeezed her once. "Ye really arenae hurt? I'm sorry ye had to deal with him for so long."

"I'm fine." She poked him in the side. "Stop changing the subject."

"The vicar?"

"We've already been living in Scotland together for well over a week. Another fortnight, and even Lord Brougham's Act won't object."

But he was shaking his head. "*Three* weeks, Treasure. We must wait until after yer birthday." When her eyes went round, he hurried to explain. "Yer inheritance is *yers*, Jade. I might own a share in Thacker Shipping, and I hope ye'll no' object to me being a silent partner—"

"I *do*," she interrupted, and when he winced, obviously thinking she meant she still objected to having to take on a partner, she softened her tone. "I don't want you to be *silent* any longer, Cam. If you're to be my partner, I want the whole world to know what a smart, thoughtful, caring man you are."

"Ye...ye really mean that." His eyes were searching hers, and he sounded...awestruck.

"I do. And the fact you care about me enough to want the world to know you're not marrying me for my inheritance..." She shook her head, then pushed herself up once more to brush a kiss across his lips. "I love you, Cam. Will you marry me?"

The grin which split his expression was earth-shattering, mind-numbingly beautiful. *Dimples*. Would their children have dimples? For the first time, she found herself looking forward to a future in which other people had control of her life.

And she couldn't be happier.

"Aye, Treasure," he drawled, his lips dropping toward hers. "I accept. I'll make ye my bride."

EPILOGUE

"I CANNAE BELIEVE ye arseholes actually came!"

Cam was beaming as he slapped his palm against the backs of his best friends. Keith Oliphant—who was built like a brick—didn't move, but Malcolm Forbes was jolted hard enough to spill his drink, and turned to scowl as he reached for his handkerchief.

"I had to come," he said blandly, patting at his cuff. "I wouldnae have believed Cam MacKay could be married, if I hadnae seen it with my own eyes. Besides, I promised Brom a visit to the London Zoo."

Smiling, Cam settled between his friends as they watched their wives socialize with Cam's family—*both* of his families—and Jade's friends. "Have ye been already? What did Brom think of the hippopotamus?"

Malcolm rolled his eyes as he readjusted his jacket. "We're going tomorrow, and the lad's in alt over the prospect of aquatic mammals and their *leavings*. I told him we werenae bringing a sample home."

On Cam's other side, Keith grimaced. "I was going to invite

myself along, since Carlotta's planning on spending the day with her mother, but now I'm reconsidering."

"Ye would rather spend the day with yer pink mother-in-law than myself and my son?" Malcolm asked with a raised brow.

"If it comes down to my mother-in-law versus hippo shite, I'm going to have to give it a long and serious consideration."

Cam, who had spent some time with the Dowager Duchess of Cashingham, shuddered slightly. "Hippo shite, definitely."

Keith hummed, his arms crossed in front of his chest. "Will there be snacks? I'll go if there will be snacks."

"Oh, for fook's sake!" Malcolm drained the rest of his drink. "Sometimes I feel as if I'm the only adult here!"

"That's an *aye* to the snacks, then?"

Cam was already chuckling. Not just at his friends' banter, but having them stand up beside him at the altar was a blessing. It was just that, since Jade had asked him to marry her, he'd been filled with the most wonderful sense of…peace. As if he knew, now that she was part of his life, everything would be fine.

And since she'd said the words this morning, binding their futures together, he'd been grinning like an idiot.

"Thank ye both for being here," he blurted, nudging Keith with his shoulder. "It means a lot to me."

"Aye, of course." Keith didn't look at him, which is how Cam knew he was embarrassed by the praise. "Besides, we had to visit Carlotta's family. And I needed to do some promotion in London for my new boxing school."

"Dinnae lie." Cam's grin turned teasing. "Ye love me."

"Well…ye're aright, I suppose."

"Arsehole," Cam cheerfully quipped.

"Prat," Keith shot right back.

Malcolm was shaking his head. "Children, children. Must I separate the pair of ye?"

"For fook's sake, Colm, ye find out ye're a da, and suddenly ye go all serious and boring on us?"

Before Malcolm could sputter out a response to Cam's teasing, Keith grunted. "He was always serious and boring."

Cam's laugh was more a snort. "Do ye recall that time we convinced him the head master's horse could do arithmetic? And he was studying for that Latin exam and didnae want to be bothered, but we dragged him out to the stables?"

"Och, aye!" Keith began to laugh as well. "And Crowe was hiding in the next stall, and he and James had that system worked out with the apples and the carrots, and…"

His remembrance trailed off as his chin sank to his chest.

Cam sighed. "Aye, I miss them too."

"I miss James," muttered Keith. "No' Crowe."

"I miss them both," admitted Malcolm. "I didnae expect to, no' after what Crowe did, but…" He shrugged. "I ken ye were closest to him, Cam, but it's been strange, kenning he's no' locked up any longer."

Suddenly, Cam wasn't feeling quite so jubilant any longer. He shifted his fists to his plaid-covered hips. "I ken it's my fault James is dead—"

"Nay," Keith immediately denied. "Crowe had a darkness we could all see, and reason to want James dead."

"And if I had kept my mouth shut, it would never have come to pass," Cam reminded him.

Malcolm shook his head. "Ye cannae ken that for certain, Cam. There was so much anger there."

This was his wedding day…which meant tonight was his wedding night. He shouldn't be thinking of Crowe MacLeod, and what his plans were now he was out of prison.

Blowing out a breath, Cam scrubbed a hand over his face. "Aye, ye're right. Still, I confess myself pleased to ken we've no' heard anything more from him. Or the papers."

"No news is good news?" murmured Malcolm.

When a man had reason to want revenge, Cam was glad to know he was on his way north. Away from Jade and everyone he loved. From what little they'd been able to determine from the articles they'd read, Crowe was heading home to Skye.

"Good riddance, is what I say." Keith nodded emphatically. "I dinnae ken how the man was released early, before serving his sentence...but if he wants to spend the rest of his days on Skye, stewing in his own guilt, then I'll make a point to never go to Skye."

Cam felt one corner of his lips curl wryly. "Remind me no' to piss *ye* off, Keith. Ye hold a grudge like no one can."

"Och, ye piss me off plenty," his friend replied with a teasing grin. "I just *like* ye. Besides, I need someone to translate all of Malcolm's foreign mutterings."

"I dinnae mutter," muttered Malcolm. "*Ye* just failed Latin."

"Aye!" Keith agreed cheerfully, smacking one fist into the opposite palm. "Nae need for it!"

They were all surprised by a throat-clearing, and turned to see Cam's butler standing there with a silver tray...which held a single envelope.

"A letter?" It was highly irregular to be interrupted for just a single letter, but on the other hand...the last time this had happened, Cam had learned he'd been married. Only not really. He was scowling when he snapped, "This is my wedding day!"

"Yes, milord," intoned the older man, looking highly uncomfortable. "But I know you and the gentlemen might want to see this together. It's the postmark, you see..."

Malcolm took pity on the servant and reached for the envelope. "It's from the Isle of Skye," he declared in a surprised murmur.

The trio of friends gathered around the letter, which was

addressed to "Cameron MacKay" and laid in Malcolm's hand like a strange, foreign insect.

"Go on," urged Keith. "Open it. Seems too lucky to receive it *now*, when we were just discussing…"

Malcolm shook his head. "It's no' Crowe's handwriting."

Of course Malcolm would remember something so specific as the handwriting of a man none of them had seen in almost a decade. Taking a deep breath, he reached for the letter and slit open the envelope with fingers which only shook slightly.

It was a single piece of paper, only two sentences, in an elegant feminine scrawl.

DEAR MR. MACKAY,

If you <u>ever</u> cared for your friend, Johnathan MacLeod, please come at once to Dunvegan Castle. He does not realize how much he needs you.

YOURS IN FRIENDSHIP,
Lady Honoria Lindsay

"WHAT THE HELL?" muttered Keith.

"Do ye need me to read the bigger words for ye?" Malcolm asked blandly. "Dunvegan is the seat of the clan—"

"I fooking *ken* that!" Keith jabbed his finger at the paper. "What do ye think it means?"

"And do ye suppose we all received them?" When they glanced at Malcolm, he shrugged and continued. "This was sent to yer home, aye? Lady Honoria obviously didnae ken ye're planning on selling this house soon, since ye're married, but does that mean she sent one to

Forbes Farm and Oliphant Castle? We're Crowe's friends as well."

Keith scowled. "I dinnae care if he needs my help. He *murdered* James. I'm no' forgetting that."

"I cannae forget that," Cam agreed as he tapped the letter against his palm, "but I owe him an apology for my part in that tragedy."

"I thought ye were trying to avoid him!" Keith growled, folding his arms across his chest in what seemed suspiciously like a pout. "Now ye're running toward him with open arms."

Cam waved the letter. "That was before *this*."

His burly friend shook his head. "I'm no' wrong, aye? This is *the* Honoria, right? James's sister? The one who caused the mess in the first place?"

"It was hardly her fault." Malcolm was slipping on a set of spectacles—his mother and new wife conspired to keep a pair in the breast pocket of each of his jackets—and reached for the letter. "But aye, unless there are two Honoria Lindsays gallivanting around the Highlands, this plea is from the eldest daughter of the Duke of Exingham, and James's sister."

Her other sister, Melanie, was Lady Marlowe, and one of Cam's best clients. *Ex*-clients. He was officially retired, after all. A small smile tugged at his lips as he remembered he was going to spend the rest of his days pleasuring only *one* woman.

But Malcolm was clearly responding to an argument from Keith. "All I'm saying is, if *she* can beg for help for Crowe, who are we to deny it?"

Keith groaned, but at that moment, a burst of laughter from across the room dragged Cam's attention away from the mysterious letter. His bride—his new wife—was standing with her aunt and Cam's younger siblings, who'd been thrilled to journey south for the wedding. As he watched, Jade reached out and adjusted the collar of Cam's half-brother—his father's heir—and the lad blushed crimson.

Cam grinned, knowing she had the same damn effect on him.

And the letter was mysterious as hell, aye, but today... today he had more important things to do.

"Colm?" Without turning back to his friends, he tapped the letter in Malcolm's hand. "Investigate this, would ye?"

His friend's response was immediate and expected. "Dinnae call me Colm. But, aye." He sighed. "I suppose ye have better things to do than be distracted by Lady Honoria."

"No' *what*, but *who*." Cam caught Jade's attention across the way, and when he winked, was gratified to see her slight blush and answering smile. "Think it's too early to sneak away?"

Keith's fist slammed into Cam's shoulder. He'd likely intended a nudge, but The Battling Bastard's blows were still legendary, and Cam turned to scowl at his friend.

"I had such plans, Cam!" Keith bemoaned. "I was going to make ye pay for all the times ye mocked me for falling in love—"

"Or no' kenning how to fook a woman," added Malcolm.

"Or offered to hide under the bed and give pointers." Keith sighed and rolled his eyes. "But now that I *see* ye here, mooning over Jade—she's perfect for ye, by the way—I've lost all sense of vengeance."

Malcolm jerked his chin. "Go on. Fetch yer bride."

Grinning hugely—both at the order and the knowledge his friends supported him, Cam gave a mock salute. Then he strode across the floor, determined to sneak his bride away from all this, and show her what she truly meant to him.

PERHAPS IT WAS THE CHAMPAGNE. Jade wasn't used to the sparkling temptation, but she'd accepted a second glass for the toasts, and now she felt as if laughter was going to bubble up out of her at any moment.

Or perhaps that was *joy*. Joy at finally knowing this man was *hers*.

"Have I told you I love you?" she murmured playfully as she untangled her fingers from his and slipped her arm through his, hugging it against her breasts. "Lately?"

Cam hummed and halted his urgent hustle along the upstairs hallway. "Now that you mention it…" He stared off into space, as if considering. "No' in the last hour."

Knowing perfectly well he'd been chatting with his friends for the last hour while she'd been entertaining their guests, she giggled. "I love you. There, does that count?"

Turning to face her fully, her new husband lowered his lips toward her neck. "I suppose so," he murmured, kissing that sensitive spot above her collar. "And I should tell *ye* how I feel, hmm?"

She was distracted by the feel of his lips under her jaw, as she tilted her head to one side. "I—yes…*mmm*…"

When he chuckled, she could *feel* his smile. The sensation made her chest feel all bubbly and light again, but when she opened her mouth, all that emerged was a moan, and he took her earlobe into his mouth and tugged slightly.

Who would've thought an *ear* could be an erogenous zone? Cam, apparently, based on how quickly he'd found hers.

Perhaps there was an entry in *A Harlot's Guide to the Forbidden and Delightful Arts* which she had missed.

Unlikely.

It was, after all, one of the books the pair of them enjoyed reading together.

For the articles, of course.

They'd spent the last weeks here in London, preparing for their lives together. They would live in her townhome, sell his, and offer his staff the choice to transfer to The Cottage. Cam had arranged a construction team to work on it, and he assured her that by the time they were ready for their delayed honeymoon, the place would be fully modernized, with six bedchambers and space for servants.

She was strangely excited about the idea of filling those bedrooms with friends and guests and bairns, as Cam called their future children.

"Treasure, I love ye," he was saying, his lips caressing all her sensitive areas, and one arm tight around her back. His other hand was already cupping her breast through the thin blue silk of her wedding gown. "Ye've made me the happiest man."

She arched into his touch, not even caring they stood in the middle of the hall, where anyone might spy upon them. "Not as happy as you've—Cam!"

His thumb and forefinger had found her nipple and rolled it. "Och, aye. Happy birthday, my love."

Her smile finally burst forth, a reminder of yesterday's adventure. Cam had stood beside her, his hand on the small of her back, as she'd signed the papers which made *Gung Gung's* fortune hers. Now Thacker Shipping was safe, and she owed it all to Cam.

The fact he'd waited to marry her until after she could claim her inheritance—therefore making it *hers* to bring to the marriage—had meant the world to her. He really understood her.

And she'd be sure to thank him, once she was done being...distracted.

Moaning low in her throat, she threw her arms around his shoulders, dragging him closer. She felt him grin against her lips, and when he squeezed her breast, she instinctively thrust her pelvis forward, cradling his hardness.

He was driving her mad, but two could play at that game. Still holding him, she slowly ground her hips against him, loving the way the motion brought much-needed pressure to her aching core. In response, he jerked forward as well, sudden enough to cause her to stumble.

They might have fallen, had he not slammed his palm against the wall behind her, catching her. Not one to pass up an opportunity, however, Jade pressed her arse against the wall and dragged him down to her lips once more.

With his hands bracketing her shoulders, she felt confident in wriggling against him, urging him to deepen the kiss, to tease her breathless.

With a growl, he dropped his hands to her hips and twisted. She wasn't sure exactly how it happened, but her shoulder smacked into a framed painting on the wall, and his hip smashed against a small table with some sort of vase on it.

Dimly she noted the sound of glass shattering.

"*Fook*," he murmured. "That was my grandmother's."

"Not anymore!" She shouldn't be laughing—their guests likely thought they were trapped in a life-or-death struggle with a thief, or something—but she was so tightly strung, she felt as if *something* had to release.

When they slammed back against the wall, and the unfortunate painting finally broke its moorings and dropped to the ground with a thunderous crash, she couldn't help her bark of laughter.

Which quickly turned to a gasp of need, because at that moment, Cam wrapped his fingers under each of her arse cheeks, and *lifted*.

It was technically impossible for her to wrap her legs around him the way she wanted—to ride him, to pulsate against him—in the silk gown.

But that didn't mean she couldn't try.

He was holding her upright, stumbling along the hallway, while she grasped at him, trying desperately to somehow get even *closer* to him. When he smacked against another table, destroying something else which sounded expensive, he released her mouth long enough to curse. Then the pair of them were stumbling through the door to his bedroom.

Thank *fook* he had the sense to kick the thing closed, or they would've made love there in full view of anyone who happened to walk by.

As it was, they fell onto the bed in a desperate tangle of buttons and ties and how in the *world* was his sporran actually attached? Where the hell was the buckle?

Eventually, he pushed himself off the bed, and his kilt fell away from his hips. Since Jade was lying there—swollen and aching and dazed with need—she reached for him with a sound of protest.

But he chuckled and padded toward a chest of drawers. When his back was to her, she hurried to kick herself out of the rest of her clothing, marveling at how adept the pair of them had become at removing—

Her brain stopped working when he turned back to her, holding something long and thick and *very* familiar.

With a wicked smile, he strolled toward her unhurriedly, preceded by his erect cock. Jade wasn't sure which she wanted to look at more; the gorgeous sight of him completely bared for her eyes, or the imitation penis he carried.

"Do ye remember this?"

"Of course." She grinned naughtily, holding her arms out in silent invitation. "I was wondering what you'd done with that."

He slid into bed beside her. "I want to hear ye call it by its name, Jade. I want to hear ye say what ye want me to do with it."

Her cheeks warmed at his authoritative tone, but she trusted him implicitly, and knew he was preparing her for untold pleasure. So she smiled up at him.

"I want you to use that dildo on me. The way I used it on myself."

"*In* ye."

It was the certainty in his tone which had her moaning when she lay back against the pillows. "*Yes.*"

His lips were everywhere, until she was squirming under his ministrations. Her nipples were particularly sensitive, a fact he loved to take advantage of. He grazed them with his teeth, sucked on them until she gasped his name, begging for release, and only then did he turn his attention to the little pearl of her pleasure.

Ai-ya, but this was even better!

She could feel her own desire dripping from her core as he lifted her knees and hooked her legs over his shoulders. He turned his attention to her folds—stroking, teasing, caressing —with both his fingers and his tongue.

Just when she was *certain* she couldn't take the torture any longer, his mouth closed around her clitoris, and she felt something hard and cool probing her entrance.

It was the knowledge of what he was doing to her, more than the actual sensation, which pushed her over the edge with a desperate gasp. As the dildo slid into her, his teeth grazed her most sensitive spot, and her orgasm burst over her in a deluge.

She screamed his name. Of course.

The dildo felt not dissimilar to his cock, but it wasn't quite as good. So before her core was even done pulsing, she opened her eyes to find him gazing down at her with a satisfied grin.

"Cam," she gasped, her body still quaking, "come to me. Make me yours."

"Ye are mine," he bragged. "Now and forever."

But she felt the dildo slide from her entrance, as he shifted himself between her legs.

Instinctively, she hooked her ankles behind his calves, allowing her knees to fall open, beyond ready to feel him slide into her, to make them *one*.

To her surprise, he hesitated, then held the dildo up between them, a wicked gleam in his eyes.

"So, ye're no' as fond of this as my cock, eh, Treasure?"

"It's perfectly acceptable." She tried to keep her tone light, as if she weren't desperate for him to slide home. "And I'm certain I can make use of it if we're ever apart. But I need *you* now, husband."

The way he clicked his tongue—vaguely mocking—made it clear he was being silly when he said in a sad tone, "I just dinnae want its feelings hurt, ye understand."

Holding his gaze, she grinned naughtily and lifted her head off the pillow just far enough to reach the dildo. She stuck out her tongue and raked it along the long ivory length, tasting her essence in the tool's shimmery coating.

Cam's eyes had gone wide. "God Almighty, Jade," he whispered hoarsely, his gaze on her mouth. "I've never wanted another woman the way I want ye right now."

It was her turn to grin proudly. "And you never will. Now, come to me, please, husband."

The dildo fell beside them on the mattress, and he slid home.

They both gasped in unison as the now-familiar sensation of *fullness* enveloped Jade, and she found herself grinning as he began to work against her.

Perhaps it was the knowledge of the power she'd held when she'd surprised him. Perhaps it was the fact she hadn't been quite fulfilled with her first orgasm. Perhaps because it was her wedding day.

Whatever the reason, she wasn't surprised to feel the pressure building against her core again.

With each thrust, he sent her closer, higher and higher. She realized she was breathing in small, frantic gulps, and he was grunting with each plunge.

Grunts shouldn't be erotic, but these were. Jade found

everything about this man to be arousing, erotic, and—*Ai-ya!* She was close again!

Their lovemaking was desperate, achingly so. She needed this as much as she needed her next meal, her next breath. And it was the knowledge she loved this man, which made it so.

Suddenly, he froze, and instinctively she tightened her hold on him. He reached between their bodies, his thumb unerringly finding her clitoris, as he thrust twice more.

And she felt herself constrict around him, urging him on.

"Come for me, Jade," he commanded.

And as always, she did.

Ai-ya, her pleasure exploded again, just as she felt the warmth of his seed spilling against her womb. Dimly, she felt him continuing to move, but her orgasm rocked her, forcing surprised mewls from her lips as she spasmed around him.

It was a lifetime later when he rolled to one side, bringing her with him, cradling her against his chest as she concentrated on just breathing.

"That was..." She couldn't form coherent thoughts. "Cam..."

"Aye, Treasure," he drawled, his big hands splayed across her chest. "Aye."

Despite her shortness of breath, she pushed herself up on her elbows, curious to see if he looked as satisfied as he sounded.

Satisfied? No. He looked *smug*. Preening. Immensely proud of himself.

Her lips twitched. Well, she supposed he had every reason to be. "You really are quite a talented gentleman, aren't you?"

He stacked one hand behind his head, smiling arrogantly. "Glib. Well-spoken. Charming."

She poked him in the side. "Those are just different ways of saying *good with your tongue*."

Chuckling, he closed his eyes. "Aye, I am, are I no'?"

Well, she could tease him just as well. "You know, when I wrote to Honoria, looking for a solution to my *problem*, and she convinced her sister to give me your contact information, I knew I was going to be spending the night with a man who was good with his tongue."

Cam hummed, as if interested, but didn't open his eyes.

Smiling now, she dragged her fingers down his chest, marveling at the firmness of the muscles beneath her touch. In the last weeks, they'd cleared out one of the parlors at her home, and used it to spar. She intended to allow her membership at the London Fencing Club to lapse, since she had the only partner she'd ever need now.

"Yes, indeed," she continued in a mild tone, as if she weren't planning wickedness. "I fully expected The Scot—that was you, of course—to teach me *all sorts* of naughty skills and tricks. I wanted to learn all about my body, and I did."

She said this last part as she slowly dragged her fingers down one of his inner thighs, and had to hold back her smile as he squirmed beneath her touch. Since she was watching, she couldn't miss the way his cock sprang to life, twitching in time to his heartbeat as it slowly began to harden once more.

His arse shifted. "What—what sorts of things?"

"Oh, things about desire and reactions…" She shifted so she was leaning down toward his hips. "And how I taste."

The way he groaned indicated he absolutely knew what she meant.

"But there's still a few things I don't know."

Her breath caressed his semi-erect cock now, and she saw his arse shift impatiently. "Like—like what, Treasure?" When she wrapped her hand around the base of his shaft, his breath whooshed out of him.

"Like this."

With that, she licked from the base of his cock to the tip, and his head and shoulders came off the bed.

His expression was a mixture of shock and longing and disbelief. "What are ye doing, Jade?"

Feeling positively powerful, she settled herself between his legs and gave him a wicked grin. "Learning, my love."

Those were the last words she spoke for a while.

AUTHOR'S NOTE

AUTHOR'S NOTE
On historical (in)accuracy

The 1880s were a fraught and perilous time when it came to that most pertinent and important part of this story: Cookie cutters.

That's right, my friends. Cookie cutters *did* exist, and our heroes and heroines weren't left to hand-cut their hearts and birds and gingerbread men all by their lonesomes. In fact, cookie cutters have been around for a long while; in the 1500s, bakers in Germany were commissioning carved wooden figures and designs to use with their dough. There's even speculation that the ancient Egyptians used similar molds to shape their sweet cakes.

So why in the fook is poor Cam stuck carving a dick out of sugar cookie dough with a knife? Because I couldn't find a single record of naughty cookie cutters that far back in history. I'm sorry.

So Cam and Jade are forced to draw and cut out their own boobs and buttocks and whatever else your imagination involved. **But!** Never say I don't love you. Because we live in the modern world, here's my favorite set of dick cookie cutters. Bonus: fornicating couple cookie cutters.

You're welcome.

Now, on to more historical inaccuracies.

I know this is going to just *gut* you to learn, but (*lowers voice*) Scrabble and Twister weren't around in the Victorian era. Scrabble was invented, to no one's surprise, during the Great Depression in the US, and officially marketed in the 1930s. Doesn't that just sound like something people did in the Great Depression? Twister, on the other hand, was developed smack in the middle of the 1960s. And I don't think I could name another game which screams "1960s!" more than this one, am I right?

But kudos to you, if you were able to identify the games as Cam and Jade are reading the instructions. Actually, that entire scene took place because I took a dare that I couldn't stick the word "twister" into the book...and it kinda grew from there.

Look, by this time, I'm pretty certain you don't read Caroline Lee RomComs because you're a stickler for historical accuracy.

Okay, moving on: For those who recognized the London Fencing Club, or the Viscount Shelbourne and the Duke of Northwich (oh, and also Master Beltrande)...well, a gold star to you! They're characters from Scarlett Scott's *Lady Wicked* and *Lady Brazen*. We chat daily, and love finding ways to make our worlds overlap. (I assume you've read her books, because she's a far better writer than I am. If you haven't...well, go start with those two, and prepare to fall in love!)

As far as the fencing scenes in this book, it might surprise you to learn I *do* have some experience stabbing pointy bits of metal into other people (*in sport!* I'm not a violent person!)...so they're as accurate as I could make them, without being—you know—completely boring. I *did* have to add in a description of Cam's fencing outfit, because OMG can't you just see him in scarlet leather?

As Cam points out to Jade, there *were* really active women's fencing associations in the 1880s, and some famous female fencers. *Their* outfits tended to be outrageous, but it was a valid form of Sport, so the more outrageous ladies did it.

However, I really like the idea of Jade, with her unusual upbringing, preferring to spar against men. Also, I'm a complete sucker for a cross-dressing plot (check out my *The Sutherland Devil*).

Speaking of her unusual upbringing, I'll say what I say in each of my books which feature a character who doesn't identify as solely Caucasian: Britain in the 1800s was a colorful, beautiful, and diverse place. People from all over the world resided and visited there, and it's silly to believe our stories feature only one race.

I'm sure you know a bit about the history of the East India Trading Company, which was founded in 1600 to basically monopolize trade to India, Southeast Asia, and China. It worked, *huzzah*, making a lot of English dudes very wealthy. They also, understandably, caused a lot of trouble in lands where—let's be frank—people weren't too keen on the English strolling in and taking resources.

By my reckoning, Jade was born in the middle of the Second Opium War.

As you can probably guess by the name, this was the second time British troops were sent to China to force the legalization of the opium trade and open access to the country for their merchants. Yep, traders like Jade's dad weren't permitted to trade with Chinese merchants all willy-nilly, and Britain didn't like that.

I won't go into the history of China in the Victorian period, but just note that relations between Jade's father and her maternal grandfather would've been tense...which is what makes the eventual marriage of John and Meilin Thacker so special.

Speaking of marriage, we absolutely have to chat about Lord Brougham's "Cooling Off Act". Isn't that just the best name ever for a new law? Lord Henry Brougham was a reform-minded Lord High Chancellor (who was instrumental in abolishing slavery in the Empire) who went on to reform the marriage laws.

Look, I seriously doubt this is the first romance you've read set in nineteenth-century Britain, right? Good, that means I don't have to go over the whole concept behind Gretna Green marriages (like I had to do with my husband when I pitched this story to him and he told me I was nuts). You know that the idea of eloping to Scotland to be married "over the anvil" by basically any guy wandering past (officially called "irregular marriages" and performed in front of two witnesses) is basically *the* biggest trope of Regency romance.

And by the 1850s, it had become a real nuisance.

Essentially, thanks to a law passed in 1754, anyone in England or Wales under the age of twenty-one couldn't be married without parental consent. Bummer, huh? Well, in the 1770s, the toll road tootled (it's a technical term) on up across the border with Scotland, *where the law didn't exist*, and now we've got a way for all these young lovers to be married. Yay!

Except...there were plenty of not-so-great uses, too. I mean, romance is well and good, but there's a *reason* parental consent is required if there's a bunch of teenaged hormones and stacks of money involved. The most famous case of an unscrupulous man coercing an under-aged heiress into marriage is the Shrigley abduction, and OMG it's just a flaming shit-show of a story we don't have time for here. (But if we meet at a convention, I will absolutely order a whisky and give you all the juicy details.)

So in December of 1856, stuffy old Lord Brougham manages to pass what comes to be called "the cooling off act", which essentially requires anyone who wants to get married in Scotland to have been residing there for twenty-one days prior to the marriage. This is similar to the idea of the banns being read in the couple's home parish, right?

Except.

(And I love this.)

After almost a century of being *the* marriage destination for young English lovers ("the Las Vegas of Britain" as my husband declared, in the midst of my attempted explanation), the people of Gretna Green were having None Of That. There's tales of locals offering their home to young lovers, or farmers allowing couples to live in their barns/fields, for the requisite three weeks...and then vouching that the couple was now able to marry in Scotland.

How cute is that?

Thank fook Lord Buthert didn't know about that, huh?

Okay, this Author's Note has gone on for far too long (#SorryNotSorry), but I hoped you learned a bit. As always, it should be clear that my books aren't here to give you a history lesson...you have to stick around 'til the end to get the good stuff!

I mean *history*, not the sex, you degenerate.

And really, anyone who names the villain of the book "Buthert" can't be trusted to take things seriously.

But as far as serious goes...

Please tell me you're ready for Crowe's story? Let's be honest, *I'm* desperate for Crowe's story. I love Keith, Malcolm, and Cam, but Crowe just burrowed into my heart and now I *need* to know what his secret is. Why did he kill James? How'd he get out of prison?

If you're a sucker for tatted-up bad boys hiding emotional scars, then hang on to your reading glasses, my friends...*The*

Sinner's Tempting Captor is waiting for you! Keep reading for an excerpt!

As always, I want to invite you to join my **reader group**, where you'll get to help name characters, check out covers, and watch all the random videos I think are funny. Or, if that's not your pace, sign up for my newsletter and get some free books from me. Feel free to do both!

Oh, and if you enjoy reading spicy historical romance and hanging out with others who do as well, come check out the Historical Harlots Facebook group!

And now...what's going on with Crowe?

SNEAK PEEK

SNEAK PEEK

From *The Sinner's Tempting Captor*

The door slowly creaked open, and Honoria realized she'd forgotten how to breathe.

As soon as there was enough space, a man stepped through —or rather, was pushed, judging from the way he turned to glare at the two guards who followed him, each armed with clubs, and one carelessly dangling a set of shackles from grimy fingers.

The prisoner in the middle rubbed at his wrist, as he slowly straightened and faced the courtyard, blinking in the same dim afternoon sun which had caused her to squint after the inner darkness. How often was he allowed outside, to see the sun? Judging from the way he tilted his face back, as if welcoming the weak glow, not often.

It was that motion which allowed her to really *see* him for the first time, and Honoria sucked in a breath so quickly she went dizzy.

Crowe.

It was him. But...it wasn't.

The man she'd once thought herself in love with had been lanky, certainly, with high cheekbones and dark brows, which she'd always thought looked a bit like wings.

This man... This man was nothing like the well-kempt, quiet boy she'd once known.

The prisoner she was about to take into custodys was still tall, still dark-haired...but his hair was well past his shoulders, knotted in locks which fell around his temples and full beard. His shoulders were wider, his wrists...

She swallowed. Beneath the ragged cuffs of the too-small prison uniform, Crowe's wrists were scarred and muscular. His knuckles showed too much abuse, and she wondered, if she opened his fist and turned his hand over, what calluses she'd find on his palms.

And how they would *feel*.

It was right about then she realized she was ogling the hands of a murderer, *in public*, and dragged her gaze back up to his face. Only to find his eyes open, and staring back at her.

His bright-blue gaze was as shocked as she expected.

Beneath the bush of his beard, she saw his lips form a word which *might've* been "Honoria." It might've *also* been "Good God" or "I have an itch" or "I miss chocolate." But she suspected "Honoria" was most likely, considering the misguided reason he'd killed her brother.

He didn't speak, and she couldn't think of anything to say except, "Hello, Crowe," which she absolutely could *not* say in front of the warden. So she inclined her head in greeting.

At that moment, one of the guards prodded him with a club, and he must've been taken by surprise, judging from the way he stumbled forward, then turned to growl wordlessly at the man.

The other guard lifted a heavily booted foot and casually slammed his heel into the back of Crowe's unprotected knee.

Honoria gasped at the violence and was already moving as Crowe grunted and dropped to the ground, catching himself on one knee and both palms. When he lifted his head, staring right at her with impassive eyes, she jerked to a halt and forced herself to take a deep breath.

Nothing will be served by allowing these men to believe he means anything to you.

Nothing would be served by allowing *Crowe* to think he meant anything to her.

Nothing would be served by allowing *herself* to think he meant anything to...

You are particularly bad at lying to yourself.

True.

And that likely would've been it, had the first guard not stepped forward and grabbed Crowe by the locks at the back of his head, yanking him upright.

He stumbled to his feet, and then Honoria was there, in front of him. She wasn't certain exactly how she'd managed that, but as the guard tossed aside his hold on Crowe, she was there to meet him.

Inside she was screaming *What are you doing? Stop! Do not touch him!* But somehow her right hand rose of its own accord.

And cupped his cheek.

It was a simple gesture. She couldn't even feel his skin, beneath her glove and the thick, coarse beard.

But as her hand touched his face, she saw him shudder, saw him shut his eyes, saw him swallow.

And knew then that she was doing the right thing.

Because she'd seen the same expression on Laird MacLeod's face when she told him of her plan: part dread, part gratitude, part desperate hope.

And although no one in her family would understand her

actions—she herself barely did!—she knew she was doing the right thing.

Here was one father and son, at least, whom she could reunite in time.

It wasn't until his eyes opened, carefully neutral, that she realized she was still touching him. She jerked her hand back as if scalded, afraid that movement betrayed her as much as the first one.

Perhaps it did, because as she stepped back, the warden stepped forward. "My lady, it was a pleasure doing business with you."

She forced her shoulders to straighten, forced her chin up, even as she turned to the rotund man. "Mr. Warden, thank you. I shall report your helpfulness to my father." There, one more hint he was doing a duke's bidding. "Are we clear here?"

The man bowed mockingly, one hand gesturing toward the door in the outer wall. From the corner of her eyes, she watched Crowe's gaze follow hungrily.

"As you have taken control of *the asset*, we no longer need to worry over his well-being."

Well-being, indeed. She managed not to snort derisively, even as she switched more of her attention to Crowe. At the warden's words, his head had jerked around, his eyes narrowing thoughtfully as he contemplated their meaning. Even now, he had to be wondering why the authorities of Dunworth Penitentiary would be relinquishing their control over him.

And, judging from the way his gaze was flicking silently between the guards and the impressive door to freedom, she knew what his next move would be.

Well, think again, sir!

She didn't go through this much trouble, this much heartache, this much *headache*, just to have him bolt at the first sign of liberty.

No thank you. You're mine.

Trying to maintain an air of nonchalance, as if bribing murderers to freedom was something she did every day, Honoria shifted to put herself between Crowe and that door, even as she began to nonchalantly loosen the straps of her reticule.

In order to distract from her movements, she cleared her throat, and holding Crowe's gaze, asked the warden, "As I understand the process, you will leave us?"

There was the sound of grumbling, then she saw the man make a gesture to the two guards. Crowe himself turned a sharp glare to watch the pair of thugs roll their shoulders, nod, and step back through their door.

Then the warden bobbed another mocking bow. To Honoria's surprise, he turned to Crowe and winked. "From here on out, you're someone else's problem, you lucky bastard."

Crowe stared back impassively.

The man, who'd clearly been hoping for some kind of reaction, scowled as he hooked his thumbs in his waistcoat pockets. "Good luck, my lady," he said, before turning and stomping toward the door to the administration wing.

And then Honoria was left alone in the courtyard with Crowe MacLeod, the man she'd once known. The man who'd killed her brother. For her.

She saw the exact moment he realized it, too. His eyes flicked from the door to one of the windows, to her, and back to the outer door. He'd always been full of coiled energy, prepared to spring in an unexpected direction. Nine years in prison hadn't changed that.

But now he looked more than capable of knocking her over on his way past.

Fumbling slightly, she shoved her hand into her reticule and tried not to breathe too obvious a sigh of relief as her fingers curled around the butt of the revolver.

"Do not do something you will regret, Crowe," she cautioned, and the man jerked as if she'd struck him.

Before her eyes, his expression—which he'd held so impassive, even as he'd growled a warning at his guards, even as they beat him into the dirt—turned to anger.

No, not *anger*. Downright *loathing*.

And that loathing, virulent, vengeful gaze switched from her to the door behind her. The door which, to him, must represent freedom.

Well, she couldn't have that.

Reminding herself she was doing this for his own best interest, she pulled the revolver from her bag and aimed it, unshaking, at his chest.

Granted, the only reason her hands weren't shaking were because her knees were doing enough shaking for her entire body, but still. She was proud of the overall effect.

Crowe's gaze dropped to the barrel of the revolver, and he stared at it for a long moment. When he looked back at her, she wondered—hoped?— that was a glint of amusement in his blue eyes.

For the first time in nine long years, she heard him speak. It wasn't the voice she remembered—more like a hoarse rasp —but it was *his*. "What…" His chest expanded, as if he paused to consider his words. "What in the fook is this?"

"This?" Lady Honoria Lindsay smiled tightly and gestured toward the door with the barrel of her gun. "This is a kidnapping."

What?

I know, right? You're going to adore Honoria as much as I do—as much as Crowe soon will—trust me! This is a book you won't forget: an enemies-to-lovers romance a decade

in the making, with angst, revenge, a snarky teenaged pick-pocket, some epic naught scenes, and more laughter than should be legal. Buckle up, buttercup, for *The Sinner's Tempting Captor,* the last book in *Those Kilted Bastards,* and free in Kindle Unlimited!

ABOUT THE AUTHOR

Caroline Lee has been reading romance for so long that her fourth-grade teacher used to make her cover her books with paper jackets. But it wasn't until she (mostly) grew up that she realized she could *write* it too. So she did.

Caroline is living her own little Happily Ever After in NC with her husband, sons, daughter Princess Wiggles. She thinks it's important to note that she made it all the way through grad school without knowing how to touch-type (she taught herself to type only a few years ago and APPARENTLY lesrned imcorrectly--*learned incorrectly,* a fact which she's only now realizing, as other authors point and laugh). Caroline adores rodents, goes through laptops like Pez, and never met a whisk(e)y she didn't like. She's also pretty funny in person. Promise.

You can find her at www.CarolineLeeRomance.com.

OTHER BOOKS BY CAROLINE LEE

Want the scoop on new books? Join Caroline's Cohort, an exclusive reader group! Or sign up for my mailing list by texting "Caroline" to 42828 to get started!

Steamy Scottish Historicals:
Those Kilted Bastards (4 books)
Bad in Plaid (6 books)
The Hots for Scots (8 books)
Highlander Ever After (3 books)
The Sinclair Jewels (4 books)
The Highland Angels (5 books)

Sensual Historical Westerns:
Black Aces (3 books)
Sunset Valley (3 books)
Everland Ever After (10 books)
The Sweet Cheyenne Quartet (6 books)

Sweet Contemporary Westerns
Quinn Valley Ranch (5 books)

River's End Ranch (14 books)
The Cowboys of Cauldron Valley (7 books)
The Calendar Girls' Ranch (6 books)

Click **here** to find a complete list of Caroline's books.

*Sign up for Caroline's Newsletter to receive exclusive content and freebies, as well as first dibs on her books! Or if newsletters aren't your thing, follow her on **Bookbub** for a quick, concise new release alert every time she publishes a book!*

65487958R00126